DARK SIDE
OF GLORY

by
BERTA W. SWAN

ZONDERVAN PUBLISHING HOUSE
GRAND RAPIDS, MICHIGAN

DARK SIDE OF GLORY
Copyright © 1969 by Zondervan Publishing House
Grand Rapids, Michigan

All rights reserved

Library of Congress Catalog Card Number: 79-89518

Printed in the United States of America

DARK SIDE
OF GLORY

1

Rodgers Madden woke early his first day home. The sky outside his window was leaden. He stared at it; impossible to predict, yet, what kind of a day it would be. His watch showed four twenty. He sighed. Too early to get up, but he was not sleepy. He lay still on his back, his long body stretched full length and relaxed under the sheet.

He smiled and thought, *I'm a minister. At long last. The Lord's servant.* He felt the familiar presence of God and closed his eyes as his thoughts became prayer. He was on the threshold of his life's work, just out of seminary, excited and anxious.

Rodgers prayed until he felt at peace. When he opened his eyes, the sky had lightened. Five o'clock. He turned on the bedside lamp, reached for the small Testament on the night stand, and began to read.

At seven o'clock he got up. The sun was bright. He looked down on the garden at the rear of the house. This was June and the flowers made an explosion of color. He could hear the hum of the power mower. Turning from the window, he stumbled over a carton of books on the floor. He'd unpacked his bags before he had gone to bed but the books were still boxed. There was a large bookcase in the room, ample space if he cleared out his old boyhood collection. He decided to unpack his books even though he might not be home for long.

Rodgers was getting hungry. He dressed and crossed to the bureau to brush his hair. He had to stoop to see his reflection in the mirror, now set too low for him. He'd remount it when he had time. His thick, light brown hair had been cut recently and stayed in place with a minimum of effort. Even brows, a shade darker, accented olive-green eyes. His features were strong and serious.

He didn't go directly downstairs, but instead went up to the third floor, to the suite occupied by his great-grandmother. He went through the sitting room to her bedroom, knowing she hadn't gotten up yet. She always had tea and toast brought in around eight.

She was asleep. Rodgers went quietly over to the bed and stood looking down at her. His great-grandmother's skin was unbelievably translucent, the veins showing clearly. She was old and frail with snowy white hair. But she was a dynamic woman; advanced age had not changed that. Her deep brown eyes were still capable of snapping with fire. Rodgers loved her dearly. There was a bond between them that he had never felt with his parents.

Elizabeth Madden opened her eyes slowly and stared at him. With recognition, a warm glow came to her face.

"I'm sorry I woke you," Rodgers apologized.

She struggled to sit up and he lent a hand. "Don't apologize. Each morning I wake, I'm lucky." She gave him a radiant smile. "Or perhaps unlucky. Depending upon your viewpoint, I guess."

Rodgers adjusted the pillow behind her back and smiled. "Let's say you're lucky. May I get your tea?"

"In a few minutes. First I'd like to talk to you. Have you time?"

"For you? Of course."

"Well, you'll be a busy young man now. I wish I could have attended your graduation."

"It's all right. Dad and Mom didn't come either, you know."

"How do your parents feel?"

"We haven't talked."

"You will," she said. She looked at him directly, looked *into* him. "Don't let them back you down, Rod."

"No. I've come too far to back down."

"You told me you were called to the ministry. Do you still feel that?"

"Yes. I was called."

"Even so, it's never easy, Rod. There will be temptations."

"I know."

"Do you have a church?"

"Not yet."

She sighed. "If I had been a man, I'd have chosen the ministry."

He smiled indulgently. "I don't think not being a man has stopped you."

She laughed. "Do you mean I preach?"

"I mean you are one of His best servants."

"Thank you, but I know what I am. If I squeeze in under the gate like Peter Rabbit in Mr. Macgregor's garden, I'll be satisfied."

"I believe Saint Peter will be glad to open the gate for you, dear."

She stirred against the pillow and grew pensive. "I believe Christ Himself comes to meet us. What do you think?"

"Yes, I believe that. Otherwise there would be fear and I'm sure there is none."

She smiled. "I don't think we ever know dying, do you?"

"No. I think we are only aware of Eternity, and that we are finally and completely Home."

She beamed at him. "You *are* a minister! God bless you, Rod!"

He grinned down at her. "You couldn't be a little prejudiced, could you?"

"Certainly not!"

He laughed. "How about that tea now? I'll have a cup of coffee with you."

"All right. You may bring it up."

To avoid waking the rest of the family, Rodgers took the back stairs down to the kitchen. He found the cook already there. His mother changed help frequently and he didn't know this particular servant. He smiled as he spoke to her.

"Good morning. I'd like to get a cup of coffee for myself and tea for my great-grandmother. Keep on with what you're doing. I can find everything."

9

"Yes, Mr. Madden. The coffee's on the stove and that's Mrs. Madden's tea there in that silver pot. I'll get the cups down for you."

"Don't bother. I know where they're kept." He hated to be waited upon. He was better able to get down the cups than she and he couldn't stand there and watch her do it for him. His mother disagreed with him; she said he didn't know how to handle servants. And she was probably right.

He poured the coffee and tea, got out sugar and cream. The cook brought a tray and placed the things on it.

"There you are now, Mr. Madden. Can you carry it up all right?"

"Yes. Thank you."

"What time would you like your breakfast?"

"Whenever the rest eat."

"It's never regular on Saturdays."

"Oh. Well, around eight thirty then."

"Yes, sir. How do you like your eggs?"

The tray was getting heavy. "It doesn't matter. Scrambled. Bacon, toast, and orange juice—if you have it."

"Oh, yes, sir, we have everything," she said, a bit affronted.

"Well—thanks." He retreated hastily with the tray. He hadn't meant to offend. For a moment he felt uncomfortable about it but by the time he reached Elizabeth Madden's room, he'd forgotten the incident.

"You forgot the toast," his great-grandmother said.

"Oh—yes, so I did. I'll get some for you."

"Never mind. Your mother has a new cook and hasn't had time to train her yet. By the time she has her trained to her satisfaction, she'll quit."

Rodgers laughed. "Probably. And I can't say I'd blame her."

"You're too easy though, Rod," Elizabeth Madden said soberly. "The Madden men were always weak. But with you it can be different. You are a man of God. None of the rest belonged to Him."

Rodgers shifted uncomfortably.

"You think I'm judging them, don't you? At ninety-one, I have the right to judge a little."

"No," Rodgers said.

"Yes," his great-grandmother argued. "Or do you believe in the new morality—everything goes?"

"No, you know I don't believe that."

"Then you have to preach about sin and evil, don't you?"

"I have to preach the Gospel," he countered.

"All right. You can begin here at home. Alicia's wild. Your mother exercises practically no control over her."

Alicia was approaching twenty-one. She was five years younger than Rodgers. They'd been devoted in childhood but he had seen little of her in the years he'd been away at school.

He frowned. "How do you mean she's wild?"

"I'll let you see that for yourself."

"Very well. If she's wild, I'll speak to her."

"She may not let you," said his great-grandmother grimly.

"Alicia and I could always talk to each other. I don't think that will have changed."

"I hope you're right." She set her tea cup aside. "It's time I rested a little more, Rod. See you later?"

"Yes. Later. Rest now." He kissed her and left the room.

He went down to the kitchen for a hot cup of coffee and carried it through the spacious downstairs rooms, out to the terrace. The sound of the power mower had ceased but he could see the gardener clipping the hedge at the far end of the garden, along the property line. *Hard working old soul,* thought Rodgers. He stood beside the railing and looked out with quiet contentment on the early morning scene.

The sliding glass door behind him opened and he turned to see his mother step through, gingerly lifting the long skirt of her housecoat.

He smiled. "Good morning. May I get you a cup of coffee?"

Her smile flashed briskly on and off like an automatic signal. "Thank you, dear, but Marie will bring it. That's her duty."

Rodgers didn't comment.

"Have you seen Gran this morning?" his mother asked.

"Yes. I sat with her while she had her tea. Then she wanted to rest so I left."

"Yes. Well, she is getting old. She sleeps more than she used to. She seems quite alert though, don't you think?"

"Yes, she does."

Marie brought the coffee on a tray and set it on a low round table.

"Will there be anything else, Mrs. Madden?"

"Not just now, Marie, thank you."

"Mr. Rodgers is having his breakfast at eight thirty. Would you like yours then, too?"

"Yes. That will be fine."

Marie went in, carefully sliding the door after her. Rodgers looked at his mother as she sat down to pour her coffee. Even first thing in the morning every hair on her golden head was in place, her make-up perfect, not a chip in the manicured nails. He didn't think he'd ever seen her when she wasn't impeccably groomed. It gave her a varnished look, he noted. She was in her late forties. The blonde hair was dyed, of course, and he thought it gave a harsh, unflattering look to the features age was trying to soften.

Helene Madden glanced up and surveyed her only son critically. "You seem pale, Rod, and thinner. You haven't been fasting or some such ridiculous thing, have you?"

He deliberately snuffed out the irritation that flared in him. "No, Mother, I haven't been fasting, just studying hard."

She shrugged and turned her attention to the garden. After a few moments' critical observation, she said impatiently, "Just look at that! He's puttering away the morning down there! These beds all need weeding; the grass hasn't been fertilized. What does he *do* all day?"

The peace of the terrace was shattered. Rodgers sighed restlessly and wished he could have gone directly to a parsonage.

"Sit down," his mother said, "and talk to me. We haven't seen you since Christmas, you know."

"I know." He sat down across from her at the low table.

"More coffee?" she asked.

"No, thanks. I've had two cups already."

"I suppose there's nothing anyone could say to you now——" she began.

12

"No. There's not."

"Your father is very disappointed, Rod. He'd counted on your going into the law firm with him."

"He's known for three years that I'm not."

"We thought — that is, we hoped — you might change your mind."

"No, I haven't. I won't."

"It's not that we have anything against the church. You know we always attend ourselves. It's just that——"

He got up. "Please, Mother. I've made my decision; you'll just have to accept it whether you agree with me or not."

"Rod! You're being almost disrespectful!"

"I'm sorry. I don't mean to be, but I have to live my own life and make my own decisions."

"Where do you think you will go? What church, I mean?"

"I don't know yet. There'll probably be invitations to preach from several churches before I get a call from one of them. I hope to be settled by fall. September, maybe."

"Dr. Broyles could use an assistant. Our church has grown so that it's really become more than one man can handle."

"Um hm," Rodgers responded noncommitally. The First Presbyterian Church was more sophisticated than he cared to handle for a few years.

Helene Madden changed the subject. "We usually go to the club for dinner on Saturday night. We don't have to go—that is, we can give it up while you're here——"

He lifted his brows. "Why should you give it up?"

"But—will you be able to go with us? I'd hate to go off and leave you here alone. On the other hand, I wouldn't want to ask you to violate any vows you've made."

"I can have dinner without violating any vows," Rodgers said. He guessed her meaning.

She looked at him in consternation. "Rodgers, I don't understand you." She got up and walked to the railing, then turned to face him. "My own flesh and blood. Named for me. And yet you've become more and more a stranger. You're not like me, nor are you like your father. A bit like Gran, I suppose."

A great deal like Gran, he thought. *We are the only ones who really know the Lord.* Neither of his parents understood his call to the ministry. Their attitude was a cause of deep sorrow to him.

"Mother, I won't embarrass you," he said. "I don't carry a soap box with me or break out suddenly into extemporaneous sermons."

"Rodgers, you needn't take that tone with me," she admonished.

Alicia stepped out onto the terrace just then, interrupting them. "Rod, good morning! Welcome home."

"Hello, Alicia," Rodgers said, smiling.

Mrs. Madden said stiffly, "Excuse me, I'll let you visit with your brother, Alicia. I'm sure he will prefer your company to mine."

Alicia lifted her brows when their mother had gone into the house. "What was *that* all about?"

"Nothing. How've you been, Sis?"

"Oh, all right. You look well." She surveyed him with a critical yet admiring eye.

"Yes, I'm fine."

Alicia was holding a large glass of orange juice. Rodgers, growing thirsty in the warm sun, took the brimming glass and drank from it. He choked and set it down hastily. It was heavily spiked with liquor.

Alicia's laughter pealed. "Serves you right! No one asked you to have any."

"When did you start this?" Rodgers asked sharply.

"Darling, don't be so stuffy," she said airily.

"I'm not being stuffy. When did you start drinking in the morning?"

"Morning! You make it sound as if I'm an *alcoholic!* There's just a little gin in there."

"There's a *lot* of gin in there!"

"It picks me up."

"It does not. It's a depressant."

"You're a depressant! Look, Rod, don't preach. Just don't preach to me!"

He had never heard her talk that way before. She had stood

14

by him when their parents had opposed his seminary training, and he had thought she was in favor of his plan to enter the ministry. His great-grandmother was right; Alicia *had* changed.

She turned abruptly away from him, her slender back straight as an arrow. She was a pretty girl, browned from long hours in the sun. Her pale blonde hair fell nearly to her shoulders and her eyes were a deep blue. She reached down to pick up the orange juice from the table where Rodgers had set it. The twist of her shoulders and the arrogant, challenging stare she gave him goaded him. Before she could take a sip from the glass, he took it and flung it onto the stone steps below the terrace.

Alicia caught her breath with a startled gasp, then wheeled quickly into the house. Rodgers leaned against the railing, feeling almost sick at his stomach. He had handled her all wrong. Getting angry had not helped. He should have exercised more control over his own emotions.

Marie came to the door.

"Your breakfast is ready, sir, and your father is downstairs. He would like to see you right away."

"Thank you," Rodgers said, and followed her inside.

2

Rodgers paused in the doorway to the formal dining room to draw a bracing breath. His father rose from his seat at the head of the table and came toward him.

"Rod! Welcome home! How are you?"

"Fine, thank you, sir. And you?"

"Fine, fine. Sit down."

Rodgers sat at the side of the long table. His mother was seated at the other end. They were unnecessarily spread out, but it was the way the Maddens always dined.

"You're looking well," observed Harvey Madden.

"He's too thin," Mrs. Madden commented.

"Oh, he'll fill out. Give him some good home cooking." He turned to Rodgers. "Son, I don't mean to rush you, but I have to be at the office at nine. I wanted you to come along with me. I'll show you around and introduce you to my staff." He laughed. "Staff! There's just my secretary and a young law student who helps out after his classes. But I'd like you to come."

"I'm sorry, Dad. I'd like to another day, but I can't this morning."

"Why not?"

"I have some calls to make."

"Calls?"

"I want to talk with the other Presbyterian ministers in town."

"Oh. I see. You haven't given up that idea then?"

"Idea? No, I haven't given it up. I'm a minister."

"You're a lawyer."

"I *was* a lawyer, or I studied law."

"You passed your bar exams."

"Yes. But that's all over. It was the wrong career for me."

"Was it? Are you sure about that?"

"Absolutely."

"Well, I don't intend to argue with you. But I do intend to try to get you to change your mind."

"I'm sorry you feel that way," said Rodgers. "I'm afraid you'll be putting us both through some rather unpleasant discussions."

"They needn't be unpleasant, do you think?"

"Perhaps not. Depends on how hard you intend to press."

"Well, we can talk about this later. Now, your mother and I would like to say how glad we are to have you home."

"I'm glad to be home," Rodgers said, not entirely sure he was sincere in saying it.

"Good, good. Things are going to work out, I'm sure." He gulped the last of his coffee. "I've got to be going, Rod. I'll see you tonight. You're going to dinner with us?"

"Yes. Thanks."

"Not at all."

Rodgers made several calls on local ministers and then later in the afternoon drove into the country. Coming to a white frame Presbyterian Church, he turned in at the graveled drive and drove around to the back. It wasn't likely that anyone would be there on a Saturday afternoon, but he'd remembered this little church and now felt drawn to it.

The front door was locked, but he found the side door open. Glancing in, he saw that the sanctuary was empty. Rodgers looked about indecisively, noticed a cemetery, and walked over to it. It was cool there, with a slight breeze blowing gently through the trees overhead. He strolled about aimlessly, reading the names and dates on the old stones, and then sat on a bench to rest. The quiet joy he'd known in the early morning returned to him. He bowed his head and began to pray.

Looking up presently, he saw an old man standing before him.

"I didn't mean to disturb you, son," the stranger said apologetically.

"You didn't disturb me," Rodgers assured him.

"My name's Wickham. Wilbur Wickham. I've been pastor of this church for over thirty-five years."

Rodgers shifted over to make room on the stone bench. "I'm Rodgers Madden. Won't you sit down?"

"Thank you. At my age one is always ready to sit, I'm afraid."

Rodgers smiled politely. The old man said, "What brings you to the cemetery? A loved one buried here?"

"No, no, I just wanted to come to the church."

"I see," said Wickham. "Well, I come here frequently myself. It's a peaceful spot. And I have loved ones here—my wife and two children."

"I'm sorry," Rodgers said quickly.

The old man smiled gently. "Oh, it was a long time ago. Nearly thirty years. They died of typhoid fever. Lots of folks died of typhoid in those days, but now you hardly hear of a case." He looked at Rodgers. "I tend to run on, it's so seldom anyone stops by. Perhaps you'd prefer to sit quietly." He started to rise.

Rodgers detained him. "No, don't go."

The old man stayed. He didn't speak again and Rodgers knew he was waiting for him to speak, if he wanted to.

"I'm a minister," Rodgers said finally. "Just starting out. In fact, I'm waiting for my first call to a pulpit. I graduated from seminary yesterday."

The old man laughed. The sudden understanding broke the ice between them. "Well, you really are brand new, aren't you!"

"Yes. A little scared, too."

"I can imagine. So was I at your age. The fear will quickly pass. He keepeth thee. 'The Lord is thy keeper; the Lord is thy shade upon thy right hand. The sun shall not smite thee by day, nor the moon by night. The Lord shall preserve thee from all evil: he shall preserve thy soul.'"

"I believe that, of course," said Rodgers.

"But you are still troubled."

"Yes. There are personal problems. My parents are very opposed."

"To your being a minister?"

"Yes. They'd hoped I'd be a lawyer. I studied law."

18

"And you graduated from seminary, too?"

"Yes."

"But you haven't decided yet whether you want to be a lawyer or a minister?"

"I've decided. They just won't accept my decision."

"I see."

Rodgers grinned wryly. "It sounds childish, doesn't it?"

"Yes, I'm afraid it does."

"I'm old enough, I should know my own mind."

"Then stick by your decision."

"That's easy to say."

"Have you been called by the Lord to be a minister?"

"I thought so."

"You aren't sure?"

"I don't know. There's so much opposition."

"There always is. It's never easy. If you want an easy time, you're in the wrong job."

"I don't expect an easy time," Rodgers said shortly.

"All right, son, maybe I'm being a little rough on you. But if you expect me to talk you into being a minister, I can't do that."

"I know."

The Reverend Wickham stood. "Come into the church with me."

Rodgers followed him to the small chapel. The sanctuary was cool in the growing dusk of evening. The wooden benches, sedate pulpit, cross upon the altar, and flowers ready for the morning service all soothed the young minister's troubled spirit.

Wickham glanced at him. "Feeling better?"

Rodgers sighed. "Yes, I am. Thanks."

Wickham went to the organ and began to play softly. "What's your favorite hymn?"

"O Love That Wilt Not Let Me Go."

Wickham played it without looking up the music. "Go ahead, sing it, Rodgers."

"I don't sing very well."

"Doesn't matter. 'Make a joyful noise unto the Lord.' "

Rodgers laughed. "Is that how you interpret that Psalm?"

19

"It's one way. Go on, sing!"

Rodgers began the first verse of the hymn.

> *"O Love that wilt not let me go,*
> *I rest my weary soul in Thee,*
> *I give Thee back the life I owe,*
> *That in Thine ocean depths its flow*
> *May richer, fuller be."*

Rodgers paused and said earnestly, "That's been the theme song, the prayer of my life." He closed his eyes and without the music to accompany him, repeated the third stanza:

> *"O Joy that seekest me through pain,*
> *I cannot close my heart to Thee,*
> *I trace the rainbow through the rain,*
> *And feel the promise is not vain,*
> *That morn shall tearless be."*

Wilbur Wickham joined Rodgers in singing the last verse:

> *"O Cross that liftest up my head,*
> *I dare not ask to fly from Thee,*
> *I lay in dust life's glory dead,*
> *And from the ground there blossoms red,*
> *Life that shall endless be."*

For a moment after the last notes died away, they were silent. Then Wickham stood up from the organ and asked, "Would you like to preach here for me in the morning?"

"I—you have your sermon prepared, haven't you?"

"Yes, but I can use it another time. I've preached so long that I would welcome a rest one Sunday. My congregation would appreciate a strong, young voice, too. How about it?"

"All right. If you really want me to."

"I wouldn't have suggested it otherwise," Wickham replied.

"Do you want to give me a topic?"

"No. You choose your own topic and prepare your sermon. I'll look forward to hearing it."

Rodgers took Wickham's hand in a firm grasp. "Thank you, sir. I'll try to do a good job."

"I'm sure you will."

Rodgers skipped dinner with his parents at the country club. He needed the time to work on his sermon. He went to his room and unpacked his books, then decided he might as well clear out the shelves and put them up.

It was nearly nine o'clock when he finished this task. He took his Bible, a notebook of sermon ideas and outlines, and a couple of commentaries down to his father's library to study. A few minutes later, realizing he'd had no dinner, he went out to the kitchen and fixed a sandwich. He ate it and drank a glass of milk while he worked.

Rodgers took as his topic Psalm 24:1. "The earth is the Lord's, and the fulness thereof; the world, and they that dwell therein." These were farming people; a sermon built around this topic could be readily understood by them. He labored happily over his task, conscious of the Spirit of God guiding him. Presently he laid his pen aside and bowed his head, moved to prayer.

When his father and mother returned from dinner, his father opened the library door without knocking. Rodgers raised his head.

"Were you asleep?" his father asked.

"No," Rodgers replied evenly. "I was praying."

"Oh, I see." Too specific a display of piety irritated Harvey Madden, who was never comfortable with religion except perhaps for an hour on Sunday mornings. He frowned at the open Bible on his desk and at the scattered notes his son had made.

Rodgers made no move to clear the papers away. "You wanted to see me?" he asked.

His father's mouth tightened. He was a vigorous, impatient man, slightly shorter in stature than Rodgers. He had dark hair that was thinning, and penetrating brown eyes.

"Yes. If you're through with that." His gesture encompassed all the religious litter on his desk.

Rodgers leaned back easily in the chair. "Not quite. I can take a break, though. Would you like some coffee?" He got up with his empty cup.

"No coffee," said Madden. "I'll have a drink. If you don't *mind.*"

"And if I do? That would stop you, I suppose."

Madden moved over to a well-equipped bar. "Why should it? Has what *I* wanted ever stopped *you?*"

"You don't think I should choose my own career?"

Madden turned. His eyes were slightly glazed by the drinks he'd had at the club. "I thought you *had* chosen. I certainly spent a lot of dough putting you through law school!"

"I know. That was a foolish mistake."

Madden's face contorted with rage. "Foolish mistake! Do you mean to stand there and call me a fool to my face?"

Rodgers flushed. "No! The mistake was mine. Dad, you've had a good bit to drink. Let's talk about this another time."

"So now I'm *drunk!* Listen, you young pup! No sanctimonious preacher is going to come into *my* house and start telling *me* how to *live!* Even if he *is* my own son!"

Rodgers had not been blessed with a saintly temper. His father's words hurt. Anger raced through him, and for a moment he felt it fire his brain. He fought for control.

"I'm not telling you how to live," he said. "I just want you to stop telling *me.*"

Madden poured liquor into a tumbler and swallowed it straight. "Someone has to tell you; if not me, who? Your mother won't."

"Is my being a minister really this hard for you to take?" asked Rodgers incredulously.

"It's such a waste, Rod! Anybody can get up and hold a Bible in his hands and mouth a few pious platitudes. Is that all you want out of life? You have a brilliant mind! I've never told you what your I.Q. is—maybe I should now."

"I know what my I.Q. is," said Rodgers.

"Well, then, do you intend to throw all that *away?* It's a great *gift,* Rod. Can't you see that?"

"Yes, I see. I want to use the gift for God."

"Oh, for the love of heaven—you sound like a demented soap-box orator! You talk like one of these nit-wit street corner preachers."

Rodgers swallowed the bitterness in his throat. "If you'll excuse me, Dad, I'd like to finish my sermon and get to bed."

His father poured another drink and swallowed it. "Where

22

did I go *wrong?*" he cried. "For the love of heaven, how did I *fail?* Can you tell me *that?*"

"I don't think you *have* failed."

"Well, I do! I don't mind your being religious. We've always been a religious family. Your great-grandmother is a saint, but you're being a *fanatic!*"

"I don't see it that way," Rodgers stated evenly.

"Of course you don't! But you are! Sometimes I think you've lost your mind. Maybe I should consider having you committed!"

"I wouldn't try that if I were you," Rodgers said softly.

Madden turned and stared. There was a dangerous edge in Rodgers' voice. "Why, that sounded like a threat. *Were* you threatening me?"

"No. Just giving a little free advice."

"Watch your tongue now! I'm your father, you owe me a measure of respect."

"I'm trying."

Madden took an uneven step nearer him. There was a little liquor left in the glass he held. He said scornfully, "What you need, son, is a little *drink!*" and threw it in Rodgers' face.

The liquor stung his eyes and ran down his face. He turned away from his father with deliberation and sat down at the desk.

Madden stood uncertainly, then he passed his hand over his face as though to clear away a haze he could not comprehend and went heavily to the door. It closed with a soft thud behind him.

Rodgers laid his head on the desk and squeezed his eyes shut in anguish.

"O God!"

3

The library door opened again. This time it was Alicia, wearing a white lace dinner dress.

"Am I interrupting you?" she asked.

"No, come in. Did you have a nice time?"

"Oh, yes. What're you doing?"

"Writing my sermon."

"That's right, you're preaching in the morning."

"Yes."

She came nearer the desk. "Why, it reeks of whisky in here! Do you get *stoned* to write your sermons?"

Rodgers reddened. "Of course not. Some whisky got spilled."

"*Spilled?* If you weren't drinking, how———?"

"Never mind. Sit down." He smiled. "Tell me about your evening."

She grinned at him. "I think I'd rather hear about *yours.*"

"Dad and I had an argument. He'd had too much to drink, and he threw some liquor on me."

"That must have been quite an argument!"

"Yes, I'm afraid it was. Who'd you have a date with?"

"Brett Davis. He's about your age. Do you know him?"

"Yes. He was a year behind me in high school. He used to to be a little wild."

"He still is."

"Do you date him often?"

"Enough. Are you going to preach now?"

"Do you think I should?"

"It won't do any good." Her eyes narrowed. She leaned forward in her chair. "How much of a square are you, Rod?"

"I don't follow you," he said.

"How square *are* you? Do you still hold to the morals of the dark ages?"

"What makes you think the dark ages were moral?" he countered.

"All right, I don't know my history. I may have the periods mixed up, but you know what I mean."

He nodded. "Do I go for the new morality? No. I don't."

"What do you call the 'new morality'?"

"I assume you're referring to sexual morality," he said bluntly. "The idea that two people who feel some sort of affinity for one another can live together without going to all the bother of a marriage ceremony."

"Yes."

"That idea isn't new. It's as old as sin."

"Ah! *Here* comes the sermon!"

"There's a word for it in the Bible."

"Some ministers say it's all right."

"I see." He turned his eyes from her face.

"Does that shock you?"

He looked at her. "Are you *trying* to shock me, Alicia?"

She shook her head. "No. I'm only trying to be honest with you. Why don't you lecture me, preacher brother?"

"Apparently it's too late for lectures!"

"You think I'm beyond salvation?"

He faced her. "Do you *care* what I think?"

"Not really."

"Then why ask me?"

"Just curious. Rod, you pious squares make me sick!"

"I feel a little sick myself," he retorted.

"You—you——" She hit him hard across the cheek.

His hand moved on the desk. It took great effort to resist the impulse to slap her back.

She noticed the slight stir of his hand. "Well! That seminary didn't take all the fire out of you, did it!"

"It wasn't supposed to. There's such a thing as controlling your emotions."

"Oh, yes. Repression. It isn't supposed to be good for you."

"Don't you believe it! What the Bible calls sin is still sin, today as well as yesterday. Don't think you've done something noble, Alicia. You were tempted and you succumbed. It's that simple. You fell into sin. Maybe you did think of it as something else—freedom, love, expression of the true personality. I've heard it all, all the fine-sounding answers and excuses. Anyway you slice it, it comes up 'sin.' "

"Well, well, aren't you holy and self-righteous, though! Above all the human failings of us lesser creatures!"

"I'm not above sinning, Alicia. No one is. It's one thing to sin—we all do that—it's another to justify it, to think we are doing good when we are doing evil."

"Put all that in your sermon. It's too deep for me to understand. All I know is how I feel."

"How you *feel!* So, when you're hungry, you eat; when you're tired, you sleep; and when you want a man, you go after him!"

"You make it sound cheap and dirty, and it's not! You have a dirty mind, Rod!"

"Oh, *sure!*"

"Yes. You *do*. Just—just leave me alone!" She fled from the room.

Rodgers looked after her with dismay. Finally, he picked up his pen. The sermon still was not finished. He read where he'd left off, and the words blurred. He put his head down and pressed his face into the crook of his arm.

Alicia! And she still didn't think she'd done anything wrong, might even continue in it. What could he say to her? Nothing, probably, he realized. She was old enough to have her values pretty well set and she had hardened herself by her sin. Yet wasn't hope for the salvation of the most desperately lost soul at the very heart of the Gospel message?

He began again on the sermon and finished it. A measure of the joy he'd known earlier returned, but it was clouded by his distress over his personal problems. He gathered together his books and went to his room. Shutting the door, he turned out the light, then went to the bed and fell on his knees beside it. There he awoke cold and stiff-muscled, to see dawn streaking the sky. He got into bed and fell asleep, exhausted and heartsick.

Alicia came to his room in the morning to wake him.

"You'd better get up, Rod, if you're preaching."

He looked at his watch. "Yes. Thanks for waking me."

"I guess you didn't sleep well. I didn't myself."

He noticed her eyes were red and puffy. She said, "Rod, could I go with you this morning?"

"Yes, if you want to."

"I do. And could we talk now? I realize you have to hurry, but I've been thinking all night—what I want to say can't wait."

"I guess so. What is it?"

"I've thought o.er what you said last night and you're right. I've been all *wrong,* Rod. How could I have been so *blind!* I'm so ashamed! And I feel so—so dirty and foul and *evil!*" She burst into tears an flung herself down on the bed and into his arms. Burrowing into his shoulder, she wept with harsh sobs that soaked his shirt. Patiently, he patted her and waited for her to regain her composure. It was long in coming but finally she stopped crying and lifted her head. She looked at him, sobbed, and he gave her a handkerchief from the bedside table drawer.

"Here, blow. Better now?"

"Yes, much better." She sighed, wiping her eyes. "This is such a nice handkerchief. Ladies' handkerchiefs are so tiny."

"Insufficient for you, anyway."

"Oh, Rod, I've lived a lie for so long. I've tried to tell myself that what I was doing was all right, but all along I've known it was wrong. I guess that's why I struck out at you so hard last night. I wish you could wash all my sin away."

"I think you did a pretty good job of that yourself."

She laughed shakily. "I've gotten you all wet."

"It doesn't matter. Pray now, Alicia. Just put your head down and close your eyes."

"What should I say?"

"You know what to say. You haven't forgotten all our early

training from Gran. Tell God you're sorry for what you've done, and ask Him to forgive you."

"Is that all?"

"That's enough. If you truly repent, He will forgive you."

"Oh, I do! Truly! I've wanted to for a long time."

"All right, tell Him that, then."

Alicia bowed her head against her brother's shoulder and did as he'd told her.

Presently, she stood up. "Oh, I do feel better. Different. Free."

"If anyone is in Christ, he is a new creation; the old has passed away, behold, the new has come."

"Say that once more."

He repeated it. "It's from Second Corinthians 5:17."

"And do you forgive me, too, Rod?"

"Of course. Scoot now, or you'll make me late."

"Okay. I'll go get my prettiest hat on." She stopped in the doorway to look back at him. "Thanks, Rod, thanks a lot."

"Go on! I've got to get dressed!"

"And about last night — I'm sorry I slapped you. It wasn't really you I was slapping——" she broke off and laughed, for he had grinned ruefully. "Though I guess it *felt* like you, didn't it?"

"Yes, it surely did!"

"Well—I *am* sorry."

"Okay. Run on, now kid. I'll see you in a few minutes."

He was running late. He shaved too quickly and cut himself.

At breakfast his father exclaimed, "Good grief, what happened to you? You aren't going to church that way, are you, Rod?"

"I have to go. The bleeding's almost stopped."

"You look like you spend your free time brawling. Can't you manage to shave without slashing your face to ribbons?"

"I was in a hurry."

"Well, put something on it."

"Like what?"

"Like ten yards of gauze and a roll of tape!" He turned to Alicia. "I understand you're going with him."

"I wouldn't miss it. Why don't you and Mother come, too?"

"To Hollis Creek Church?" asked Helene Madden. "No, dear,

I think not. We'd better go to hear Dr. Broyles." She turned to Rodgers. "You wouldn't accept a call to that church, would you, dear?"

"They have a minister, Mother."

"Well, I'm glad of *that*. I'm sure you could do better than Hollis Creek."

Rodgers' lips tightened, but he said nothing. Alicia glanced at him and smiled her understanding.

"He could do better than being a minister at all, as far as that goes," said Madden.

Rodgers wolfed down his breakfast, glancing frequently at the time. "We've got to run, Alicia. Hurry and swallow your coffee."

"I've finished. I'm ready to go."

"Okay. I'll just run up and say good-by to Gran."

His great-grandmother was awake, propped up in bed having her tea and toast. She smiled at him.

"Well, you look nice this morning. Did you scratch your face?"

"A little."

"Are you attending services with the family?"

"No, this morning I'm preaching myself."

"At First Church?"

He shook his head. "A small country church. Hollis Creek. Ever heard of it?"

"Yes. I've seen it but I've never been inside. I wish I could hear you. Are any of the family going?"

"Alicia."

"That's good. She can tell me all about it when you come home." She hesitated, frowning, and then asked, "Have you had a chance to talk to her yet, Rod?"

"We talked last night, and this morning she prayed for forgiveness. She's a Christian now, Gran."

"You're sure about that?"

"Yes. I'm sure."

She shook her head. "These are dangerous times, Rod. Young people have always faced strong temptations, but now the country is in such a moral decline." She smiled. "Do I sound like a moldy old woman shocked by the normal behavior of youth?"

He said soberly, "No. Some of the standards of today are low. You're right about a moral decline."

"I tried to talk to Alicia. I don't think she liked it."

"Well, she and I had quite a frank discussion last night. And after this morning I think things will be different." He got up and kissed her faded cheek, crisp as fine paper beneath his lips. "You rest now. And don't worry."

She smiled. "Worrying is about the only task I'm still able to perform."

"Well, it's not a good one, you know. It shows lack of faith in Him."

"Now don't you lecture me about faith!" said his great-grandmother. "Faith is a thing I know a good deal about. Presbyterians don't like much emotion in their religion, but they're wrong. If you haven't cried out for God with the tears at the bottom of your heart, you haven't really found Him at all. But when you *have* found Him that way, there's nothing in earth or heaven or hell that can take Him from you."

Rodgers felt a thrill at her words. "Yes, that's true, Gran."

"You've found Him that way, have you?"

"Yes, I have."

"Then when you preach, remember that. Tell them how to enjoy God. The moralizing part of your ministry will almost take care of itself if you get the faith across to them."

"I'll remember that." He kissed her again and promised to stop in when he got back from church.

Alicia was waiting for him in the front hall.

In the car, she asked, "Rod, is it really all right now? The things I've done?"

He glanced at her. "If we confess our sins, he is faithful and just to forgive our sins and cleanse us from all unrighteousness."

"Where did you get that?"

"First John 1:9." He handed her his Bible. "Look it up and read it for yourself. You've been forgiven, so you must forget the sin now. Read Psalm 103:12: 'As far as the east is from the west, so far does he remove our transgressions from us.' Then go on to verses 13 and 14. 'As a father pities his children, so

30

the Lord pities those who fear him. For he knows our frame; he remembers that we are dust.' "

She looked up the references. "You recited all that letter-perfect, Rod. How do you know it so well?"

"I've read it thousands of times. A minister who didn't know the Bible wouldn't be much, would he?"

"I guess not. I wish I knew it the way you do."

"If you read and study it, you will. The answers to all the problems that plague mankind are in that Book. It's a blueprint for life, the only true guide we have, in fact."

"I'm beginning to believe you're right. Who would have thought that Alicia Madden would 'get religion'!"

Rodgers said, "You were a little misguided. I should have been around more in recent years. When you needed a big brother, I wasn't here."

He glanced at her soberly as he drove. "The future will be hard for a while, Alicia. Your friends won't understand the change in you at first, but as time goes on you'll get your own opportunity to witness."

"You expect me to convert them?"

"No. You can't do that. *I* didn't convert *you*. Through you the Holy Spirit may reach some of them for Christ. You can show them through your witness that you've found a better way of life. Some won't understand, some will ridicule, some you'll lose forever as friends. But you'll make other friends . . . . ."

"Some I hate to face again. Brett Davis, in particular."

"I know. It won't be easy. Perhaps the best thing to do about Brett is to refuse next time he asks for a date."

She shook her head. "No. That would be the *easiest* way all right. But I don't think it would be the most effective witness."

"Just make sure it is *your* witness that wins," said Rodgers, "and not his. Satan is strong, too, you know. Temptation doesn't die in your life when you accept Christ; sometimes it becomes more compelling than ever."

Alicia shuddered. "Don't scare me, Rod. You *will* help me?"

"Of course. But your surest help comes from God. He is your fortress. Psalm 46 tells us that 'God is our refuge and strength, a very present help in trouble.' "

4

The small chapel at Hollis Creek was almost filled to capacity when Rodgers got up to preach. He felt a sudden shyness as he looked out on the faces of the people, their expressions expectant as they waited to hear him. There was only one infallible cure he'd ever found for that; he bowed his head and asked the congregation to join him in prayer.

The sermon went well. The attentiveness of the people as they listened encouraged Rodgers, and he felt that God was leading him step by step as he delivered the prepared message. After he sat down the organist began the familiar hymn, "O Love That Wilt Not Let Me Go." Rodgers rose and sang with the congregation. Wilbur Wickham stood beside him. As the last notes died away he turned and touched the young minister's shoulder.

"That sermon was truly inspired, son. Thank you for coming."

Rodgers nodded. He had never known greater happiness, nor had he ever been more sure of his commission than at that moment.

"I'd like for you and your sister to join me at my house for lunch," Wickham said. "It won't be fancy, but my housekeeper always leaves something for me. It will give us an opportunity to talk further."

"Thank you," Rodgers said. He turned to his sister. "Alicia, do you have other plans?"

She smiled. "No plans at all. I'll be happy to come, Mr. Wickham."

The manse was just beyond the cemetery. After a lunch of

sandwiches, frozen salad, and coffee, the elderly pastor took his guests into the living room. Rodgers settled into an armchair with an appreciative sigh.

Wickham smiled indulgently at him. "Before you get too comfortable there, I want to show you some of my books."

Alicia excused herself with an offer to clean the kitchen and left the two ministers alone to talk. ·She sensed the rapport that was developing between them.

Rodgers was theologically closer to the thinking of the older minister than to his own peers. Wickham was delighted with his views, and it was late in the afternoon before the men could bring themselves to cease poring over old books and comparing notes on the interpretation of Scripture. Wickham apologized to Alicia for detaining her so long.

"I've had a marvelous afternoon," she assured him. "I went for a walk. I want to show Rod that old cemetery—some of the markers date back to the 1800's."

"Yes," said Wickham. "This church was built in 1905, replacing an old log structure. The cemetery is older than the church." He took Rodgers' hand. "Thank you for coming. We'll get together soon for another talk."

"I'll certainly look forward to that, sir," Rodgers said warmly.

He and Alicia strolled through the cemetery. Now and then she pointed out an interesting marker she had found.

"And there are some Wickhams here," she said. "Did you know that?"

"Yes. Mr. Wickham told me. His wife and two children."

"It was a long time ago. How did it happen—do you know?"

"Typhoid fever."

"And yet he stayed on here and carried out his ministry all these years."

Rodgers looked at her. "Why shouldn't he have?"

"Oh——" She shrugged. "Some people might have blamed God, you know."

"I'm sure Wickham doesn't blame God."

Alicia stopped walking and turned to her brother. She shaded her eyes from the late afternoon sun as she looked up into his face.

33

"That was really a good sermon this morning, Rod."

"Thank you."

"I mean—it was great. It was really great!"

He smiled, and gave a slight nod. "Thank you."

"Oh, you!" She squeezed his hand impulsively. "You were *good,* Rod. Terrific! I really didn't know you had it in you."

"It wasn't me, Alicia," he said then. "It never is the minister when a sermon goes over well."

"Oh, I know. You were inspired or something." He lifted his brows but she went on. "I *still* say you were marvelous."

"Well, I wasn't. But I'm glad the message touched you."

"It did. And this place. Haven't you guessed why I dragged you out here?"

"Not to see the old grave markers?"

"There was a deeper reason."

"All right, suppose you tell it to me."

"You won't make fun?"

"Don't you know me better than that?"

"Very well. I'm afraid to leave."

"Afraid? I don't understand."

"Ah, there, I shouldn't have told you!"

"Just explain. Do you mean that you feel safe here?"

"Yes."

"From what?"

"From sin, temptation, the crowd I was going with. From the things I've done and don't want to continue in. Don't you see?" Her eyes searched his imploringly.

"Yes. But you can't run away."

"Oh, that's easy for you to say, Rod, when you have nothing to run away from! Don't be *smug!"*

"I'm not. I have my own spiritual torments. Do you think what the family is doing to me—their opposition—is easy to shrug off?"

She looked at him. "I didn't know it was bothering you."

"It is. Very much."

"But why? If you want to be a minister, why do you *care* how they feel?"

"Alicia, they're my parents. Of course I care."

"But I wouldn't think it'd really keep you from what you want to do."

"It won't, but it does cause considerable heartache."

"You'd better not let them know you have any doubts." She sighed and started walking, scuffing up leaves with her feet. "I wish I could drop out of the old gang, never see them again."

"They aren't all that bad, are they?"

"Well, they are all rather wild."

"Alicia, are you afraid of them or of yourself?"

She glanced sideways at him. "Myself. That I won't hold out against their arguments to go on being the way I was. I suppose you're going to say I must witness to them."

"No. It's a bit too early for you to do that, I think. You may be right to drop them."

"I'd hate being a coward."

"Then stay and fight it out. That's what I intend to do."

She reached for his hand. "We'd have each other. And Gran. She's all for your being a minister."

"Yes." He smiled down. "She's all for your being less wild, too."

Alicia flushed. "I know. Rod, don't tell her how bad I really was."

"I won't tell her anything. But she's wise. I imagine she knows."

"I'm so ashamed!"

"Shame is healthy sometimes. You've repented and been forgiven though; you can forget it now."

"As if it had never happened."

"That's right."

"It seems too good to be true, doesn't it?"

"Nevertheless, it is what He has promised. 'I will forgive their iniquity, and I will remember their sin no more.'"

"I'm afraid," she confessed again.

"Don't be," he said, while feeling the tremor of his own fear. How hard would his parents press him? How strong was his commitment to Christ? Here in the shadow of this church he felt strong enough to bear anything; put to the test by Satan, as he was sure to be, would he stand up?

In the weeks that followed, Rodgers was invited to preach in other churches. Twice he returned to Hollis Creek, and always he was well received there. In mid-July Wilbur Wickham and an elder of the Hollis Creek Church named Joe Daniels came to call.

Rodgers was on the terrace with his mother when the visitors were announced. They had just finished lunch.

"Show them out here, please, Marie," Rodgers said. "And bring some iced tea for them."

Mrs. Madden rose. "If you'll excuse me, Rod——"

"Mother, wait, please. At least meet my guests."

"I hardly see the point——"

"Manners. If for no other reason," Rodgers insisted.

She stayed, reluctantly. Rodgers introduced the men to his mother and watched as she extended a cold, formal hand to each in turn. Daniels seemed uncomfortable; Wickham took it in stride.

"Mrs. Madden, you have the makings of a fine young minister here," he said kindly to her.

"So I understand. His father and I had hoped we were raising a lawyer."

"Oh?" Wickham turned to Rodgers. "You told me you studied law."

"I did, but I've decided against it. I told you that, too."

"He passed his bar exams," Mrs. Madden said.

"That's a lot to give up," observed Joe Daniels.

Helene Madden smiled. "I'm glad to find someone who agrees with me, Mr. Daniels. An education is not to be thrown aside lightly, is it!"

Daniels warmed to her attention. "It certainly isn't," he agreed. "A college degree, and in the law at that! Well, I reckon that's something to be right proud of."

Wickham said, "And yet you went to seminary *following* law school, didn't you, Rod?"

"Yes," said Rodgers, grateful for a champion. "There's no question of my going into law now."

"Not many in your position would feel that way," said Daniels. "And your father being a big lawyer himself, he could help you out."

"Exactly!" said Helene Madden. "He had planned on taking Rod into the firm. He'd counted on it, in fact."

"Young folks tend to make their own decisions," Wickham pointed out.

"And sometimes they don't know their own minds," said Mrs. Madden.

"That's true," Daniels agreed. "My own kids are that way. Don't know from one minute to the next what they want."

Marie brought the tea. When it had been served, Wickham said, "We aren't here for a purely social call, Rod. We have some business to discuss with you."

Mrs. Madden rose. "I suppose that's my cue to leave."

"No, no, stay if you'd like," said Wickham.

"Really, I have things I must do." She paused in the doorway. "Did Rod tell you, Mr. Wickham, that our own Dr. Broyles at First Church has asked him to be assistant pastor there?"

Wickham's faded eyes widened and sought Rodgers'. "No, I don't believe he mentioned it, Mrs. Madden."

"It's true. We are all quite proud of Rod." She smiled. "Good day, gentlemen."

"Thank you for the tea, Mrs. Madden," Wickham said. He waited until she was gone. "So you've accepted a call to First Church. Congratulations. Only I think you might have told me, Rod."

Rodgers walked to the railing and turned, leaning his back against it. "I didn't figure there was anything to tell you. I did receive a call from them. I haven't accepted it."

"Have you refused it?" Wickham inquired.

"Not yet. I haven't decided."

"Why not?" asked Daniels.

"I felt I needed more time," Rodgers said frankly.

"More time? What on earth for?" asked Daniels. "A fine church like that and you got to have *time?*"

"Well, that's *his* decision," said Wickham. "We'd better tell him why we're here, Joe."

"Not much point to it now," Daniels grumbled.

"He's not committed. Tell him." Wickham glanced at Rodgers. "Sit down, Rod."

Rodgers sat. "Well, what's on your mind?"

"Since you're figuring on maybe turning down First Church," Daniels said with a rueful laugh, "we thought you might consider coming to us."

"I might," Rodgers replied. "As assistant to Wickham, you mean?"

"No, as pastor. Wilbur wants to retire. But you aren't *serious?*"

"Aren't you?" asked Rodgers.

"We were. Before we came here," Daniels said.

"We didn't know then that you'd been offered the position at First Chuch," explained Wickham.

"I understand all that. What are you trying to say—that you don't want me if First Church does?"

"Naw, that's not it," Daniels protested. "We want you, but if you've got this good chance——"

"I see." Rodgers smiled. "You two are the worst snobs it's ever been my misfortune to run across."

"*We* are?" Daniels cried.

"You and Wickham. You can't conceive of a minister being more interested in your church than First, can you?"

"Can *you?*"

"As a matter of fact, I can."

"Are you saying you might be interested?" asked Wickham.

"I'd like to hear the details, yes," replied Rodgers.

"We can't pay like First Church," began Daniels.

"No, I wouldn't expect you to."

"And the manse isn't fancy. You've seen it."

"Yes. I liked it. It's more room than I'd need, actually."

"Well, it needs some repairs but there's plenty of willing hands to keep it up for you. That wouldn't be a worry. There's a housekeeper, too. She'd be willing to help you like she has Wilbur. And she won't charge you much."

"All right."

Daniels blinked. "Are you acceptin'?"

"Still listening," said Rodgers with a smile.

"Well, that's about all."

"When would you want me to start?"

"Soon's you can. We'll give you a little time to get settled before you go to preaching, if you want. Wilbur's located a room to move into, with the Kelleys."

"He needn't move. If I won't bother him, I'd rather have him stay on in the manse."

Daniels glanced at Wickham. "You two can work that out. When can we have your decision, Mr. Madden?"

"Any time."

Daniels blinked again. "You mean——"

"I'm prepared to accept your offer."

"What about First Church?"

"I'll have to turn their offer down, of course."

"You're sure about this?" inquired Daniels doubtfully.

Wickham rose. "Don't talk him out of it! Thanks, Rod, thanks very much."

"Thank *you*."

"We'll keep this quiet until you talk to Dr. Broyles," said Wickham.

"All right. I'll be in touch with you as soon as I see him. By the end of the week at the latest."

"Take your time. And let me know when you're ready to move into the house."

"I want you to stay on there," Rodgers repeated.

Wickham searched his eyes. "That isn't necessary, you know. Or customary. I'd planned to go to the Kelleys'."

"I'm sorry to upset them," Rodgers said, "but I need you. I hope you'll do me the favor of staying on."

Wickham turned away and coughed hastily. He blinked more rapidly than usual. "Of course, Rod, if you really want me. God bless you, son."

Rodgers shook hands with both men and saw them out. Mrs. Madden did not reappear.

5

It was two days before Dr. Broyles' busy schedule could be arranged to accommodate Rodgers. Even then the interview was constantly interrupted. A telephone call came just after Rodgers sat down in the large study.

Broyles leaned across his polished desk with a smile. "Excuse me, Rod. Always something. Hello?"

Rodgers waited, blotting out the call from his conscious hearing while his eyes took in details of the pastor's study. It was a pleasant room—heavy draperies at the wide windows, plush carpet underfoot, several deep, comfortable chairs for visitors. The wall behind the minister's desk was solidly lined with books. Wilbur Wickham had an adequate library; this one far surpassed it.

Broyles replaced the telephone in its cradle. "Now, then, Rod, I'll be brief. I haven't made my hospital calls yet. Your work will be mostly with the young people. I haven't taken on an assistant before this because"—he flashed a perfunctory smile—"most of our parishioners insist on coming to me anyway, and there's not a lot they'll allow another minister to do for them. But my work with the youngsters has been somewhat neglected."

"Sir, I——"

The telephone broke in. Again, Rodgers waited through a lengthy call.

"As to salary," continued Broyles, "I don't believe the session has fixed yours yet. It'll be adequate, I'm sure. And of course

40

your expenses are not too great while you are with your parents. No immediate plans for marriage, have you?"

"No, but——"

"Good, good. Wait and choose just the right young lady."

"Sir, I——"

The church secretary came in. Rodgers waited. She left after Broyles signed some letters.

Broyles glanced at his watch. "I really must be getting to the hospital. Until Miss Helen reminded me, I had completely forgotten my luncheon engagement with Fred Gilcrest. You know Fred, don't you? Good friend of your dad's. He's largely responsible for the new wing on the Sunday school building. Generous contributor."

"Dr. Broyles——"

"Rod, I'll ask you to wait on your questions, please. I really do have to rush along. Perhaps Saturday morning we can get together again—no, I'm addressing junior choir then. But soon, I promise."

Rodgers stood up. "Dr. Broyles, I came here to turn *down* the position, *not* accept it!"

"Turn *down!* What are you *saying?*"

"I don't feel this church is the place for me to start my ministry. I'm sorry. Your offer was very kind, but I just cannot accept it."

"Now see here, I understood——"

"I'm sorry. I have accepted another pastorate."

"*Another?* Where?"

"Hollis Creek."

The barest smile started at the outer corners of Broyles' mouth. "Hollis Creek? Are—are you *serious,* Rod?"

"Yes. Why?" Rodgers asked smoothly.

"Well, it—it's a small country church. I don't think you'll feel very much at home there."

"On the contrary, I feel right at home there. Do you know Mr. Wickham?"

"Is that old fella still around?" Broyles chuckled. "Yes, I know him. Slightly. Rod, does your father know about this?"

"Not yet. I'll tell him tonight. I wanted to talk to you before I let the news out."

"You'd better talk to your father, too, before you let the news out."

"He has nothing to do with my decision," Rodgers said.

"He had a great deal to do with mine," said Broyles. "I didn't think I wanted an assistant pastor here until your father pointed out some rather obvious—advantages."

"What do you mean?"

Broyles folded his hands on the desk. "Just that your father has been generous to this church. We felt we owed him a favor if he wanted it so much."

"He doesn't even want me to be a minister. Why would he want me in this particular church?"

"We didn't go into his reasons. He wanted it."

"And put pressure on you? I'm surprised you took that."

Broyles straightened and his mouth tightened. After a moment, he said, "I take a lot that you wouldn't understand, Rod. Don't judge me until you are older, until you've faced some temptations of your own."

"Well, you're off the hook. Tell him I refused your offer."

"That won't appease him."

"I'll tell him myself, then."

"Would you accept for a year or two? The experience won't hurt you and it will appease your father and Gilcrest."

"*Gilcrest?* What's he got to do with it?"

"He asked me to take you on."

Rodgers gave a ruffled laugh. "That's flattering! What does Gilcrest owe my father?"

"I didn't ask."

"There seems to be a lot you don't ask!"

"Yes. But as I said, reserve your judgment."

"Well, let me out of it. I don't want their favors. Tell them anything you want. I'm accepting the pastorate at Hollis Creek."

"I wish you'd reconsider."

"I'm sorry, Dr. Broyles. I can't."

Rodgers left, disillusioned. How could anything make a man of God defer to a man like his father? Why was Broyles so anxious to please him? The church didn't need money that badly.

Rodgers headed for Hollis Creek. Entering the empty building, he strode to the front of the sanctuary and flung himself into a pew. He bowed his head and allowed the peace of the place to soothe his disquieted spirit.

Presently, the side door opened quietly and Wilbur Wickham shuffled down the aisle.

The old minister smiled. "Hello, son. I saw your car out front. Looking your church over?"

"Not exactly. Seeking refuge."

The old man nodded. "This is a good place to find it. Any particular problem?"

"Oh——" Rodgers sighed. "I talked to Broyles. Seems he was rather compelled to take me on as assistant pastor. My father's idea."

"Hm. What did you tell him?"

Rodgers looked up. "Why, that I was coming here, of course. What else would I tell him? I don't want First Church. And certainly I wouldn't want it under those circumstances. I was a little surprised at Broyles, frankly."

"Yes, I imagine you were."

"He asked me because my father and another heavy contributor applied pressure. Can you beat that?'

Wickham nodded. "It happens. We're human, Rod. Remember that. A minister is as liable to sin and err as the next man. We're all tempted sorely, and you will be, too. Perhaps not by money and position as Broyles has been—and he *has* done a lot of good in that church. More than anyone else could have, probably. You'll have your own devils to conquer."

"I realize that."

Wickham shook his head. "No, I don't think you do, yet. When Satan climbs on your back, he'll ride you hard. The dedicated ones with stars in their eyes always attract him the most."

"You're scaring me a little," Rodgers said.

"I'm trying to warn you. Satan and I are old acquaintances. I bear many scars on my soul."

"And yet God's grace is sufficient. I'm sure you've found that true."

"Yes. But your soul will be the battleground. It can get terribly bloody. Never discount the sting of the serpent."

"But thanks be to God, who gives us the victory through our Lord Jesus Christ."

The old man's eyes were misty. "I think you'll come through all right, Rod. I shall never cease praying for you, that your faith and strength fail not in the times of testing."

Rodgers faced his father at home after dinner. He went to the library where the elder Madden was working on a brief.

Rodgers shut the door and waited until his father looked up. Then he asked, "Why'd you go to Broyles about me?"

"Who says I did?" Madden queried.

"He did. Didn't you?"

"Yes. As a matter of fact, I did."

"Why? What difference does it make to you where I serve?"

Madden shrugged. "I thought you might as well start with the best."

"Oh, no. That's not the reason. You thought I'd fail quicker at First Church than anywhere else!"

"That's ridiculous!"

"Is it? Well, I turned him down. I'm going to Hollis Creek."

"*Hollis Creek?*" His father laughed. "Now I know you're out of your mind. Or is this just to spite me?"

"No. I'd made my decision before I talked to Broyles. Don't try to interfere with me again, Dad. I mean that."

"There you go sounding threatening again. I don't believe you learned anything at that seminary except disrespect."

"For some things, yes. Respect for others."

"The Bible says to honor your father."

"In the Lord. I'm trying to honor you, but you make it pretty difficult. I must be a minister. And I must serve God where I am called."

"*Called!* You were *trained* in the law."

"And in the ministry."

"All right! Go to Hollis Creek! Go on and throw your life

44

away on that hick farming community. Just get out of here, Rod, and leave me alone!"

"Sir, if you'd only try to understand——"

"Get out!" Madden's face reddened with rage. "Just get out!"

Rodgers, his own face chalk white, turned and walked briskly from the room. In the hall, he passed his mother.

"Rod, I could hear the sound of your voices way out here. Are you and your father quarreling again?"

"Not again. Still."

"Where is Alicia? Do you know?"

"I haven't seen her."

"Her sorority has been trying to locate her. She's overdue at some meeting or other—pre-rush, I think they said."

"*Sorority!*" Rodgers laughed. "Is *that* all that's bothering you?"

"Well, dear, it's an obligation she's assumed. She ought to be there." She stared at him. "Rod, you're acting very strange."

"I know. I'm sorry, Mother. If I see Alicia, I'll tell her you're looking for her."

Rodgers found Alicia in his car. She was huddled in the front seat—a damp-faced bundle of misery. He opened the car door and climbed in beside her.

"Okay, want to tell me what's troubling you?"

She shook her head.

"That bad, huh?"

She nodded mutely.

"Well, let's see now—perhaps I can guess."

No reply.

"You went out with the old gang."

Silence.

"You tried to explain how you've changed. They didn't understand. They wouldn't buy it. You were the joke of the evening."

She straightened on the seat and looked at him. "That's almost correct. Only it wasn't the gang; it was Brett. We talked. He even listened to me. He was very patient. And then he had his say. He had an answer for everything. His arguments sounded reasonable — and he could present them unemotionally, intelligently. He made me sound like—like——"

"A fool," supplied Rodgers.

"Worse. Naive. I felt like a baby."

"Um hm. And the serpent said to Eve, 'Ye shall not surely die.' "

"What's *that* supposed to mean?"

"The devil always tries to get us to question God's Word. He plants a doubt."

"And Brett is the devil?"

"No—a tool, let's say. It won't be easy, Alicia, I've told you that."

"I didn't expect it to be easy. But I didn't expect it to be impossible either."

"It won't be impossible."

"Oh, Rod, I don't know. I'm not sure I can take it."

"Just what can't you take?"

"The loneliness. Giving up everything, and all my friends."

"You may be trying to give up more than you need to. Being a Christian doesn't stop you from living; it opens up life to you. A gloriously abundant life. It is being born again. The way of death is by way of sin, not by the way of Christ."

"But they don't *see* it that way! Brett doesn't see. No one *wants* this! It stifles!"

"No, it doesn't stifle, Alicia. Far from it. Christ's way is the very breath of life; it is sin which suffocates us."

"Who's going to believe *that?*" she countered.

"Don't preach to them. You can't prove anything by moralizing. Sell happiness. Show them that you have found a better way of life. Make them *want* it."

"Be the light of the world! My battery's dead."

Rodgers chuckled in spite of himself. "I'm afraid that's an accurate description of a lot of Christians. You can get it recharged. It doesn't happen overnight. And some of your friends never will understand, but that doesn't mean you have to go back to their darkness."

"Oh, Rod, it sounds easy when I talk to you, but then——"

"It *isn't* easy. Forget that you ever thought it would be. The way of the Cross is *hard,* but any *other* way only leads to pain, corruption, and the eventual loss of your soul. The way of sin is death, Sis. Of course, it doesn't look that way at first. Satan is the great deceiver. Many people won't realize they're spiritually dead until it's too late."

She looked at him wonderingly. "I've heard the things you're saying all my life. You make it sound so *real.*"

"It is real. It's a life and death struggle, believe me." He sighed and said, "Dad ordered me out of his library tonight. We quarrelled bitterly."

She touched his arm in compassion. "Rod, I'm sorry."

"Yes. So am I. I regret that my being a minister has become such an issue between us. Sometimes I wonder if I'm right to go on with something that so provokes him. There are other ways I could serve God, I suppose."

"Don't *you* lose courage."

He smiled. "Thanks. We'll have to help each other. We'd better go in now. Mother is looking for you. Seems your sorority is tracking you down—something about a rush party you're supposed to attend."

"I forgot all about that! I ran into Brett and decided this was the time to confess all. It's too late to make the sorority thing now. I'll explain to them tomorrow."

Affectionately, he commented, "Seems explaining is keeping you busy."

When he went with Alicia to the house, his father opened the library door and called to him.

"Rod, step in here, please. I'd like to see you for a minute."

"Luck," whispered Alicia.

Rodgers followed his father into the library. The older Madden closed the door firmly behind them.

"Sit down, Rod."

Rodgers hesitated. "Dad, don't you think we've both said too much already tonight?"

"I want to apologize for yelling at you. There was no call for me to lose my temper."

"All right. I accept your apology. I'm sorry my being a minister displeases you so much. It has never been my intention to displease you."

"I realize that. I'm disappointed, though. I can't deny that."

"So, what more is there to discuss, Dad?"

"A great deal. Please, Rod, sit down."

Rodgers sat, with a heavy sigh. "I don't know how much more of this I can take."

"Do you think I'm enjoying it? I've argued with you and I've advised, Rod. Now I'm going to do something I'd hoped to avoid; I'm going to plead with you."

"Dad, don't——!"

"I'm *begging* you, Rod! I'll go down on my knees to you, if that will help."

Rodgers pushed to his feet. "I've heard all of this I intend to listen to!"

"Sit down!" Harvey Madden grabbed Rodgers by the arm and spun him around. "You sit down there and you listen! You listen well. The next step for me is suicide!"

Rodgers' indrawn breath rasped. *"What?* What are you trying to pull?"

"I'm not joking!"

"Then you must be out of your mind!"

"Maybe. I'm desperate, I know that. I don't know where to turn, son, I'm at the end of my rope. Are you ready to listen?"

Rodgers sat down. Madden leaned on the desk. "You know Judge Green?"

"I've heard of him."

"Criminal Court Judge."

"What about him?"

"I'm getting to that. Rod, I've been highly successful. I have a good reputation, the reputation of a winner. People come to me because they know I can win."

"What's your point?"

"No man gets where I am all by himself. Most of my clients are guilty; that's why they come to me. I usually get them off."

Rodgers' eyes narrowed. "Go on."

"Judge Green has been very helpful. I've been grateful. For

48

a while he was satisfied, but he's getting old. And greedy. It practically amounts to blackmail on the present scale."

"You might have expected it would."

"I might have. I didn't. I need you, Rod."

"No, thanks!"

"You don't understand. I want to break with him. With you in the firm, I could do it."

"You can do it without me in the firm."

"No. I'm no longer a young man, Rod. I haven't the strength to do it alone. If you could come in for a little while, you could see me through this crisis. I can't pay him; if I don't get him off my back, he'll ruin me."

"For how long a time would you need me?"

"Four to six months. No longer. Handle the cases I've got pending that are due to come up before Green. I'll have to pretend illness—we can say it's my heart. I'll tell him you know nothing about our arrangement. He may hint around with you; I don't think he'll come right out and make a proposition. He knows you're a minister. Anyway, if he does suggest anything, you can turn him down."

"And after six months, what happens?"

"He comes up for re-election. I don't think he'll make it. Will you do it, Rod? Six months?"

"You're asking for my life."

"Only six months. Then you can take up your ministry where you left off. You can go to Hollis Creek. And you'll have the satisfaction of knowing that I'm on a straight path finally, and that you put me there. After all, you want to save souls, don't you? Would a delay of six months matter so much to you, Rod? Think what it'll mean to me. You have years ahead of you in which to pursue your own career."

"And if Green *is* re-elected?"

"I'll still be out of it. I promise you that. Six months is all I'll ask of you."

"Can't you tell him yourself that you don't want to go on?"

"No. Believe me, I can't. He'd never buy it. He's a vengeful man; he'd expose me."

49

"How, without exposing himself?"

"He'd do it. Rod, I wouldn't ask if there were any other way. What do you say? Will you?"

"I'll let you know. I'll have to think it over. And I need to pray about it."

Madden's lips tightened involuntarily and as quickly relaxed. "I'll wait for your answer, then. Good night." He strode quickly from the room, closing the door after him.

Rodgers dropped down into the chair at the desk and buried his head on his arms. The subtle serpent began to sting.

The following days were soul-searching ones for Rodgers. His father waited impatiently for his answer. Wilbur Wickham waited patiently for Rodgers to finalize plans to move into the parsonage and take up his duties at Hollis Creek Church.

However, events came to a head unexpectedly one Sunday in July. Before dawn Harvey Madden attempted to take his own life with an overdose of sleeping pills. Only the prompt action of Mrs. Madden in calling the doctor saved him. He was rushed to the hospital, but it was several hours before he was pronounced out of danger.

The doctor came to the visitors' lounge and drew Rodgers aside. "Let's go down to the coffee shop. I want to talk to you about your father."

They were silent until the waitress brought their coffee and left. Rodgers placed his hands around the steaming cup and said, "Okay, let's have it."

"I've known your father for a long time," Dr. Graham began. "This is the last thing I would have expected."

"Could it have been an accident?" Rodgers asked.

"You know better than that. You don't *accidentally* take half a bottle of pills. What I want to know is *why* he did it."

"Ask him."

"I have. He won't talk to me about it. Maybe he would to you, you're his son. Anyway, you've got to try, Rod. Unless we know why he did it and get help for him, this could happen again. Next time we might not be this fortunate."

"I'll talk to him."

"I think I can keep it out of the newspapers. We'll say he's had a collapse. Not a heart attack, but some strain. He will need a while to recuperate—that will explain it and yet not leave the impression that he's incapable of returning to his practice."

Rodgers gave a rueful smile. "Say in six months?"

"It shouldn't take that long. Unless your father wants the rest." Dr. Graham got up. "I have other patients to see. Let me know if you have any success talking to him, Rod."

Rodgers went directly to his father's room. Mr. Madden was asleep. Rodgers gained permission from the nurse to wait in the room. He looked at his father. The older man seemed vulnerable lying so still in bed, and Rodgers realized that he was well into middle age. Fifteen more years and he would be an old man. Resentment rose. But this! His father was really pulling out all the stops to get him out of the ministry and into law. His father stirred and opened his eyes. The nurse leaned over him solicitously.

"Mr. Madden? How do you feel? Your son is here."

Rodgers approached the bed. His father looked up at him, then said quite clearly, "May I see my son alone, please?"

The nurse glanced at Rodgers. "I'll be out in the hall. Let me know when you're leaving, Mr. Madden."

Rodgers waited for the door to close behind her. "So," he said grimly, "you couldn't wait for me to make up my mind, could you? You tried to hurry my decision."

"Is that what you think? You're wrong."

"Am I? Then why *did* you do it?"

"Because I know you don't want to come in with me. I can't fight Green alone. And I suppose I didn't want to live to see my family dragged through the mud. Green will do that. I've told you, he's a vengeful man."

Rodgers sighed wearily. "All right, Dad, you win. I'll come into the firm."

The sick man's eyes kindled fire. "Rod, do you mean that?"

"Have you left me a choice?"

"No one's forcing you."

"No? Do you think I want to live the rest of my life with your death on my conscience?"

"I'll only keep you for six months, Rod. I promise."

"Unless another crisis crops up."

"It won't. Six months. Then you can go to Hollis Creek or wherever you want."

Rodgers glanced at his watch. If he hurried he could still make the service at Hollis Creek. And then he'd have to talk to Wickham.

"Dad, you need rest. I'll be in to see you later."

"All right, Rod. Thanks for coming by, and for coming into the firm with me. You don't know what it means."

"Yes, I think I do," Rodgers said gravely. It meant the delay—or perhaps the end—of a dream. Maybe he could go back; maybe he never would. He spoke to his father's nurse and walked down the corridor. His footsteps drummed: *Why, God? Don't cast me out! Why? Why?*

"Oh, God!" he said, and did not realize he'd spoken aloud until a nurse turned to stare at him. He walked on.

The service at Hollis Creek was beautiful in its simplicity. But for Rodgers it was like salt rubbed into the wound of his disappointment. The organist saw him and changed her prelude with a smile, going into his favorite, "O Love That Wilt Not Let Me Go." Rodgers returned her smile, but the beloved words ran through his mind like a taunting laugh that mocked his desolation. "I rest my weary soul in Thee, I give Thee back the life I owe, that in Thine ocean depths its flow may richer, fuller be."

But he was leaving the ocean depths. He was returning to the world of law, to the market place.

Something his father had said several years before came to him —"You are afraid of life, Rod. You want to shut yourself away in a cloister."

That wasn't it! He wanted life, abundant Life! He had found it in Christ, but it wasn't enough for him to be a layman. He had to go the final mile. Half a loaf left him hungry still!

"Oh, God!"

Wickham looked sharply at him. So he had cried out again.

The service was over finally. He went out with the congregation and waited on the lawn for Wilbur Wickham to finish shaking hands at the doorway.

When Wickham joined him, Rodgers said, "I have to talk to you. Can you give me a few minutes?"

"That's a silly question and you know it," Wickham replied. "Do you think I'd ever turn you down? Come home with me, Rod."

They walked across the shade-dappled lawn to the manse.

"Beautiful day, isn't it?" remarked Wickham.

It was a glorious day. The sun was shining brightly through lacy trees. It was a day to make the heart sing and the spirit soar, ordinarily. It was not a day to match the dark despair in Rodgers' soul.

"Yes, I guess so," he agreed without expression.

Wickham glanced at him. "You have a problem."

They arrived at the manse and Wickham opened the door. As Rodgers walked into the quiet, neat parlor, the feeling of peace in the room eased him a bit.

"I don't know how to begin, Wilbur," he said, sitting down. "There are no words to say what I have to say."

"Let's eat first, then we'll talk, Rod. You look all in."

"I am, but I don't think I can eat."

"We'll see. I'll fix you something anyway. Stay there and rest, I won't be long."

Rodgers leaned back in the armchair and tried not to think of what he was going to say. He had gone over and over it in his mind; maybe when the time came, the right words would be there, somehow. Wickham was old and he might not understand. Rodgers felt he should not tell him all the details. He was tired and presently he dozed fitfully. When Wickham returned with the tray, he awoke.

"Sorry," the old minister said. "I believe you were asleep, weren't you?" He handed Rodgers coffee and a sandwich.

Rodgers sat up. "This does look good. I guess I'm hungrier than I thought. I forgot to eat breakfast."

Wickham smiled. "I'm forgetful in my old age, but I don't forget my meals."

"My father tried to kill himself last night," Rodgers said bluntly. "He took half a bottle of sleeping pills."

"Is he——?"

"No, he's not dead. We got him to the hospital in time." He took a swallow of coffee. "Wilbur, he did it because of me."

"How do you know that?"

"He's been despondent because of my plans to go into the ministry instead of into law practice with him. He needs me in the firm."

"That's nonsense. He can get any young lawyer, Rod. Most of them would jump at the chance to practice with a man of your father's reputation." Wickham looked at the younger man. "But I take it you've decided to go yourself. Is that what you've come to tell me?"

"I told him I would for six months, yes. Don't you see, Wilbur? I can't take the chance that he won't try this again."

"So you'll allow him to blackmail you."

"Blackmail?"

"Emotional blackmail. It's practiced all the time."

"He's in a jam. I can't explain it to you, but I have to help him. Then I can return to the ministry."

"Can you?" The keen edge of disappointment showed in his voice. He had counted on Rodgers' coming to Hollis Creek.

"He's promised me that."

"Has he? Do you think it's his to promise? You were called by God. The call may not come a second time."

"I'm not really giving up the ministry. I'm delaying it for six months."

"Jesus said, 'No one who puts his hand to the plow and looks back is fit for the kingdom of God.' "

"Wilbur, I can't kill my father over this."

Wickham quoted again, " 'Do you think that I have come to bring peace on earth? I have not come to bring peace, but a sword. For I have come to set a man against his father.' "

"Don't! Please, don't, Wilbur. I'm in agony over this anyway. I thought at least *you* would understand."

"And so I do. You're making the wrong decision; I'm trying to get you to see it." The old man wagged his head stubbornly.

"He needs my help."

"I don't know what he's told you," said Wickham, "but I can't believe your coming into the firm is the only way out for him. You've committed your life to God, Rodgers. You shouldn't break that commitment. To do so would be a grave sin."

"Ordinarily, I'd agree with you. In this case there are mitigating circumstances that demand a delay."

"No. If I were less sure of your call, I might think so. There can be no circumstance to justify your quitting, Rod; or He would not have called you to begin with."

"I'm not quitting, but maybe I was mistaken about the call."

"No, you weren't."

"How do you know that?"

"I've loved the Lord all my life, Rod, but I sincerely believe your love for Him is more intense than mine has ever been. There's something in your eyes—a radiant burning—that I've seen only once before, in the eyes of an old mission doctor I met long ago. I believe you are destined to become a great minister."

"I don't want greatness."

"I didn't mean in a worldly sense. You have the potential to receive great spiritual power. Don't turn your back on this gift, Rod. Any man can become a lawyer. Especially the kind of lawyer your father is."

"What do you mean by that?"

Wickham said pointedly, "If I were guilty, I would hire him."

"Are the guilty to be unrepresented, then?"

"He does more than represent them. You aren't that blind, are you?"

"Well, you needn't worry about *my* ethics," said Rodgers.

"Perhaps not, in the beginning."

"I appreciate your vote of confidence," Rodgers said shortly. "Could we talk about something else?"

"Certainly. What subject would you suggest?"

"Look, Wilbur, don't *do* this to me."

"I'm not doing anything to you."

"You know what I mean. Right now I need your love and support. We've been able to talk."

"I don't know anything about law."

"Then we'll talk about what you do know. I'd like to continue our friendship, Wilbur."

"That's fine. But don't think our relationship will be the same as it would have been if we'd worked as ministers together. It won't be."

"It could. If you'll let it."

"It will be you who breaks it off, Rod." Wickham put aside his plate and cup. "Do you want me to give the news to Joe Daniels? Or would you like to talk to him yourself?"

"I suppose I should."

"It won't matter. I thought you might rather not."

"Thanks, Wilbur. Don't try to hold this pastorate for me. I haven't the right to ask that of you or the congregation. My decision needn't affect your plans to retire."

"I probably won't retire just yet. It won't be easy to get someone else to come here."

"I suppose not. And yet I wanted it myself so much."

Wickham looked at him compassionately. "Yes, I know you did. You're making a grave mistake, but I don't guess there's any use in my going over and over that with you. Your will's set."

Rodgers rose. There seemed no reason or excuse to prolong his stay. He knew then that Wickham was right; he could not continue to come here. An intangible bond had been severed; Wickham no longer believed in him. Rodgers knew that this would be his deepest regret. He needed the older man now as never before.

For a moment the gazes of the two men locked, then Rodgers looked away and cleared his throat.

"Good-by, Wilbur."

"Good-by."

He walked away from the manse quickly, almost running. He drove five miles out of his way before he realized he'd taken the wrong turn out of the churchyard. Pulling onto the shoulder of the country road, he stopped. For a long time he sat staring out across the land. The afternoon was golden. There was no darkness or despair anywhere that he could see, except within himself. He had made a choice which seemed necessary, and in so doing had alienated his dearest friend.

Looking into the rear view mirror quite by chance, he was surprised to see a girl walking alone along the roadside, approaching his car. There were no houses nearby. She'd probably pass on by. He paid no more attention to her. However, she stopped beside his window.

"You goin' far?"

Rodgers looked at her. "Where do you want to go?"

"Are you offerin' me a lift?"

"If you want it."

She came around the car and got in solemnly. "I don't usually accept rides with strangers," she told him. "But I recognized you. You preach at Hollis Creek church sometimes."

"Why, yes, I do—I mean I did."

"Aren't you a minister?"

"Well—no. I'm a lawyer."

"I don't understand——"

"I trained for both; now I've gone back to law."

"Somehow, it'd make more sense the other way around."

"Well—there were circumstances I couldn't control."

She sighed. "Oh, yes. Circumstances. I know about them, all right." She looked at him. "I'm sorry that you aren't preaching."

"Thank you. I'm sorry, too."

She pointed up the road. "We're near my house. See that light off to the right? I live there. My name is Mary Jane Martin."

He turned into the side road and pulled up before a farmhouse. Mary Jane opened the car door.

"Much obliged for the lift. Won't you come in?"

"I guess not. Some other time."

"Why do you say that? There won't be another time."

Rodgers smiled at her candor. "Do you want me to come in with you, Mary Jane?"

She shrugged. "I just thought—well, it's getting on towards supper time. You could eat with us. With Ma and me; my pa's away. It won't be fancy like you're used to, but you'd be made welcome." She glanced up at him. "You were kind to me. I'd like to pay you back."

"That's not necessary," Rodgers said, "but I'll be happy to come."

7

Mary Jane led Rodgers into the house. It was plainly furnished but as clean as hard working hands could scrub. The windows sparkled in late afternoon sunshine. The shabby furniture was adorned with crocheted antimacassars.

"Ma!" Mary Jane called out. "We got company!"

Her mother came through the doorway. She was a tired looking woman. She smiled at Rodgers while pushing back strands of light brown hair with water-roughened hands.

"Ma, this is the young minister who preached over at Hollis Creek. Only now he says he's a lawyer. He was kind enough to give me a ride home so I asked him to stay to supper."

She extended a hand to Rodgers. "I heard you preach, Mr. Madden. It was a fine sermon. We're glad to have you stay to supper. My name's Eva Martin."

"I appreciate your invitation," Rodgers said. "I hope I'm not putting you to too much trouble."

"No trouble at all. My husband Tom won't be home for supper. He went huntin'."

Mary Jane sighed heavily and her mother cast a warning glance upon her that Rodgers didn't understand.

"Just make yourself at home, Mr. Madden. Supper will be on the table shortly."

"Please, both of you, call me Rod."

"All right, Rod. Mary Jane, you keep him company while I go out and dish up."

The girl sat down and seemed for the first time ill at ease.

"Why the sudden shyness?" Rodgers asked. "Do you find it easier to talk to strangers?"

She looked at him soberly. "There is something to that, you know. It'd be easier to tell things to a stranger."

"Is there something you'd like to tell me?"

"Sure. Everyone has something, don't they? Some trouble—if they only knew where to tell it."

"I suppose that's true."

She said, smiling, "Of course, if you were still a minister, you'd say 'tell it to the Lord,' wouldn't you?"

He laughed. "I probably would."

"What would you say now? Tell it to a lawyer?"

"Depends. Is it law trouble?"

Her eyes were serious. She shook her head. "No. I guess it's not law trouble. Not properly. It's about my pa. I'll tell you later. Maybe it'd help to talk to someone. And you were a minister, even if you say you aren't now."

"I'll be glad to listen. And I would probably still say, 'Tell your troubles to the Lord.' I guess I'll have to get used to the idea that I can serve the Lord as a lawyer, too."

The meal was simple—chicken, cornbread, fresh garden vegetables. There was plenty of milk to drink. Rodgers had gotten out of the habit of drinking milk. He liked it.

Mary Jane offered to help her mother after supper, but Mrs. Martin said, "No, you take Rod along to the porch. It'll be cooler there with night coming on."

Mary Jane was wearing a cotton dress and sandals. Sitting in the porch swing, her brown hair hanging loose around her thin, oval face, she looked younger than her eighteen years. Her candid grey eyes surveyed Rodgers thoughtfully.

"What are you like?" she asked. "Tell me all about yourself."

He leaned against the porch railing. "I'm not a very interesting topic. I'd rather hear about you."

"There's nothing to tell. I finished high school this spring. I help Ma out here on the farm—I'd get a job but she needs my help more'n we need the money." She paused a moment, then said, "My pa drinks. That's the problem."

He nodded. "It's a tough problem."

61

"He didn't used to. He was always a real hard worker."

"What started him?"

"My brother's serving in Viet Nam. Pa's worried about him. Ma is, too, of course, but she just takes it and goes on. You know? I think women do that better'n men. Oh—no offense."

He smiled. "No offense taken. I think you're right. Go on."

"That's all. That's where he is tonight—out drinkin'. Ma always says he's gone huntin' to explain his absences to folks."

"Where does he go to do his drinking?"

"There's a sort of tavern on up the road. I wish that place'd burn down!"

"Yes, I know how you feel. Do you want me to go get him for you?"

"No, that won't do any good. He'll come when he's ready. Then he'll sleep all day tomorrow and the work won't get done."

"I could help out, maybe."

She smiled. "I doubt you know anything about farmin', do you? Anyway, I couldn't let you do that."

"I could learn, I expect."

"No. You've got your own life and I imagine your own problems. Want me to be a good listener now and hear yours?"

He stared down at her serious young face for a moment. "Yes, I believe I do, Mary Jane." He told her about his father, except the exact legal trouble he was in.

"Rich folks can have troubles, too, can't they?" she commented.

"Definitely."

"And so you have to quit the ministry."

"Yes, but not permanently, I hope."

"Must be hard for you—wantin' it so bad."

"It is hard. I hate to wait even six months. More than anyone can imagine."

"No, I think I *can* imagine. It's hard to lose anything you love. And a man's life work is more'n a job. Maybe you are doing wrong to give it up."

"I don't think so. I can't see that I have any choice."

"You think he'd really kill himself?"

"He's tried once."

62

"That could have been play actin', couldn't it?"

"Maybe. I can't take that chance." He roused himself from a comfortable position. "Tell your mother good-by for me, and again that I enjoyed the dinner."

She nodded. "Sure."

"Good night, Mary Jane."

"Good-by."

He quirked an eyebrow. "I said good night, not good-by. There's a difference."

"I know the difference."

Rodgers laughed. "You're an odd kid. Do you know that?"

"Not so odd. And I'm not a kid. Why would you see me again?"

"I want to."

"Why?"

"Do I have to give you a reason?"

"I don't like games, Rod."

"I'm not playing games. We're friends. That's reason enough for me to come back, isn't it?"

She shrugged thin shoulders. "You're likely to find me right here on the place, if you come. Anytime."

He smiled. "In a world filled with change and insecurity, that's a comforting thought."

She put out her hands to clasp both of his. Solemnly, she said, "Good night, Rod."

"Good night."

As he drove back to town the night was clear, as the day had been. The stars were out. It was the sort of night that usually aroused a joyous response in Rodgers' soul, and even this night he was not completely immune to it.

"Thou leadest me," he said softly. "I must believe that. Oh, Father, how hard it is to change my course!"

Rodgers stopped in town to call the hospital. His father was making a rapid recovery, he was told. There was nothing to be concerned about. He drove on home and slipped quietly in the back way and up to his room. He didn't feel up to facing the family yet to discuss his change of plans.

He had to face them at breakfast, but they had already heard the news from his father. Alicia was quiet. Her eyes met Rodgers' reproachfully.

His mother said, "Your father is very pleased, Rod, over your decision to come into the firm with him. I think you have made a wise choice."

"It's just for six months," Rodgers said.

"That will be a nice trial period. Perhaps, then, you will want to make it permanent."

"You were late getting in last night," said Alicia. "Were you with Mr. Wickham all that time?"

"No. I met a girl. I stayed for supper at her house."

"Anyone I know, dear?" asked Helene Madden.

"I doubt it. Mary Jane Martin. Her folks are farmers. In the vicinity of Hollis Creek."

"Farmers? A farm girl?"

"Yes. She's very nice."

"Rod, really!"

Alicia giggled.

"Really what, Mother?" asked Rodgers.

"There are plenty of girls for you to date around here. Girls we know."

"I know this girl. But it wasn't a date."

"What on earth could you have in common with her?"

"She's pleasant. I enjoyed her company. Don't get so excited, I only met her yesterday."

"But one day is as a thousand years," said Alicia.

"I wasn't aware you knew your Bible so well," commended her brother.

"Both of you hush," said Helene Madden.

"Mother, he's too old for you to tell him whom to date," Alicia reminded. "In that *at least* he seems to have a mind of his own."

"I think I detect a dig in that last remark," Rodgers said.

"How perceptive you are this morning, brother dear."

"I can't tell anymore when you two are quarreling," complained their mother.

"Rodgers never quarrels. He gives in. Don't you, dear?" Alicia asked with a smirk.

Rodgers got up. "The trouble with you is, *dear,* that no one ever spanked you long enough or hard enough when you were a child."

She smiled again, derisively. "Well, any time you think you're man enough for the task, you're welcome to try it."

"Now, don't press your luck," he advised. "My saintly patience can be stretched just so far."

"Hush, both of you," said Mrs. Madden. "Rodgers, when are you starting in the firm?"

"Soon. I'll wait for Dad to get on his feet. He'll have to show me the ropes. Next week, I expect."

"If you're not too busy this morning, maybe you'd drive me into town," suggested Alicia.

"Sure. When will you be ready to go?"

"I'm ready now. Mother, I won't be here for dinner. I'm going to call Brett and see if we can't line up something real *wild* to do."

"Sounds like fun," said her mother absently. "Don't be out too late, will you, dear."

"No, I won't," Alicia replied obediently. Both the caution and the promise were habitual, and virtually meaningless.

Driving into town wtih Rodgers, Alicia said, "Aren't you going to make any comment on my date?"

"No."

"Really? I expected you to read me the riot act."

"Well, you're wrong. I have nothing to say."

"You don't object, then, if I line up something wild with Brett?"

"I'm sorry you feel you have to strike back at me, Alicia. I'm doing what I think's right." He glanced at her. "You could try the same."

She gave a taunting laugh. "You're knuckling under to Dad's pressure on you. Don't make it sound more noble than that. Or maybe you never wanted to be a minister; lawyers certainly make a lot more money."

"They certainly do."

"And no one expects a lawyer to be a saint."

"No, no one does."

"And so you just couldn't take it, could you?" she persisted. Latent rage surfaced. "Lay off! I've had enough!"

"Oh, ho! Thou art losing thy saintly temper, brother dear. Or in more common place terms—thou hast blown thy cool."

"Don't be profane." After a moment, Rodgers said, "All right, what did you expect me to do? He took the pills on my account, you know. Am I supposed to ignore that?"

"Did you ever ask yourself why half a bottle? If he were bent on killing himself, why not take them all?"

He glanced at her in surprise. "I thought he took all the pills he had."

"No. There was a full bottle. He took half of it."

"You're sure about that?"

"Positive. Mother had just had the prescription refilled. And I saw what was left of the pills myself. Rod, if you'd known that——"

"No, it wouldn't have made any difference. He took enough to kill him."

"Did he? With Mother right there in the same room, how big a chance was he really taking?"

"You're saying he staged this?"

"He could have."

"Well, even if he did, it's too late for me now. I've got to go into the firm because I've promised. And I've resigned from Hollis Creek."

"Will you really give up law after six months, Rod?"

"I can't answer that yet. I'll have to see how things turn out. There's a problem in the firm. I can't discuss it, but you should know I've had a very strong reason to make me willing to turn my whole life upside down. I haven't done this because it was what I wanted to do, Alicia."

"All right, forgive me, Rod."

"Instead of calling Brett, how about allowing your brother to treat you to an evening on the town?"

"You needn't do that."

"I want to."

"All right. You've got a date."

Rodgers dropped Alicia off, then drove to the hospital to see his father. In the corridor, he ran into Dr. Broyles.

"Oh, Rod! I've just heard the news. Congratulations!"

"Thank you."

"I'm glad for your father's sake. He has wanted this badly. Sorry the church is losing such a fine young minister, though."

"Thank you," Rodgers murmured.

"But say! I have an idea. Why don't you take a Sunday school class?"

Rodgers flinched. "What?"

"Teach a class. What could be more natural with your training? And you'd be fulfilling your mission, so to speak."

"Well—I—" Rodgers floundered, feeling as though a barb were twisting in him.

"You might work with the young people. Yes! That would be the very thing, I believe. What do you say, Rod? Shall I turn your name in to the superintendent?"

"No—not yet. Let me see how much time I have. I've been away from law for several years, you know; I have some catching up to do."

"Of course." Broyles smiled widely. "Nice to see you again, Rod. And keep that idea in mind."

Rodgers shut his eyes. Teach Sunday school. And the day might come when he'd be grateful for even that much to do in the Kingdom. Crumbs from the table. He opened his eyes and walked slowly down the corridor, blind with disappointment and resentment. He pushed open the door to his father's room. Harvey Madden was sitting up in bed.

"You just missed Broyles," Madden said.

"I saw him in the corridor."

"What'd he have to say?"

"I can have a Sunday school class if I want it."

"Oh! And what did you tell him?"

"That I didn't think I'd have the time."

"Sure. Why give them what they were going to have to pay for!"

Anger, violent and unreasoning, whipped through Rodgers. He

said dangerously and low, "Don't criticize the church to me, Dad. Not now, not ever. Or Broyles."

"All right. I didn't realize you were so devoted to him."

"I'm devoted to him. And to every other minister."

"Okay, I'm sorry."

"About Green," said Rodgers. "The elections for judges are in August, aren't they?"

"That's right."

"Then he's out next month?"

"Next year. August of next year."

"You'll need me a *year?*"

Madden shook his head. "Six months. As I've said. The cases I've gotten involved in with him will come up by January. Don't you trust me?"

"Just trying to get it straight. You told me the elections were in six months."

"You must have misunderstood me," Madden said. "The briefs are in my desk. Miss Hamilton will get them for you anytime you want to go by there. Read them, talk to the clients. Handle the cases any way you want; I'll leave it up to you."

"Will your clients object to having me take over?"

"They haven't a choice unless they want to get another lawyer. Miss Hamilton will explain to them that I'm ill."

"How hard are these cases? I'm inexperienced, you know."

"They aren't too hard. You can handle them. You have to, there's no other way out of this."

Rodgers went over to the window and looked out. The unsuspecting clients wouldn't be getting much for their money.

"Without Green's cooperation, what are my chances of winning in court?" Rodgers asked.

"That'll be up to you, I'd say. We'll see how much you learned in law school."

"And how much I've forgotten since."

"The library's still standing, last I heard."

8

Miss Hamilton was Rodgers' idea of a typical legal secretary. She wore a dark skirt, a tailored white blouse, heavy horn-rimmed glasses, and failed to give him any awareness of femininity. She led him into his father's office and briskly laid out the briefs on the desk.

"Is there anything else I can help you with, Mr. Madden?"

He smiled, trying to break down the air of reserve between them. "This should do it, Miss Hamilton."

"Then I'll be in the outer office if you should need me."

"Thank you."

"Oh——" she turned back. "Your desk will be delivered later this morning."

"My desk?"

"Your father ordered one for you. Didn't he tell you? You're to have the office next to this one. We've had it full of files, but we're getting it cleared out for you."

"Oh. All right. Thank you." He wondered how much she had been told. Did she know, for instance, that he only planned to stay six months?

The cases didn't appear too difficult. He concentrated on them all morning, jotting down notes to remind him of a question to ask a client or a point of law to look up later.

Miss Hamilton opened the door at noon, interrupting him.

"Mr. Madden, I'm going to lunch now, if that's all right."

"Yes. Carry on as you usually do. I'll learn the routine."

She smiled slightly and came a little farther into the room. "May I ask you——?"

He looked up.

"You studied for the ministry, didn't you? I understood———"

"Yes."

"You know, that might help you. There was a lawyer in my home town who quoted from the Bible in court. He was very successful. I think the jury thought they were doing God's will to decide in his favor."

Rodgers was repelled. Bluntly, he said, "Miss Hamilton, I don't intend to capitalize on the fact that I am a minister."

She looked surprised. "I'm sorry, Mr. Madden. I didn't mean to offend you. I only thought———"

"I *know* what you thought."

"I *am* sorry," she said contritely.

"It's all right. Let's forget it."

"No, it's not all right. I can see I have really offended you."

"Well, perhaps I offend too easily." He met her eyes. "You see, it was very difficult for me to give up going into the ministry immediately."

"Then you came into the firm because of your father's illness?"

"Yes."

"But you do intend to stay."

"For about six months."

"Oh. I wasn't told that, Mr. Madden."

"My father probably hopes this will be a permanent arrangement, but it won't be. At least," he added candidly, "I hope it won't. I plan to go back into the ministry."

As the afternoon wore on, Rodgers tried to put down a growing uneasiness concerning the cases his father had given him. They didn't seem too important, at least not important enough to warrant making a deal with Green. Several were minor offenses by first-time offenders, the sort of cases any responsible judge would have granted a suspended sentence on without being bribed to do so. Five were charity cases. The firm wouldn't receive a cent for handling them, and little if any prestige. One was a libel suit; the evidence seemed flimsy. Here, perhaps, Green's support was needed to collect any damages, but the amount asked was too small for his father to risk personal involvement in a matter that could, if found out, result in disbarment proceedings.

There was only one case that seemed to Rodgers significant: a drunken driving charge lodged against a minor in a prominent family. The offense had led to a serious accident in which a man was gravely injured. There was little doubt that the seventeen-year-old boy had been drinking—police testimony and three witnesses at the scene verified that he had been under the influence of alcohol at the time of the accident. The injured man's family was suing for seventy-five thousand dollars. Little history had been taken on the case. Rodgers decided he'd better talk to the boy and his parents right away.

He summoned Miss Hamilton. "Try to locate my sister. We're having dinner together. Tell her I'll be delayed. I'll meet her somewhere—anywhere she says—at seven o'clock. If you can't find her, leave the message at my home."

"Yes, sir."

"And get Mr. Robert Ammons on the line for me. Or his wife if he can't be reached."

"Yes, sir."

Mr. Ammons was at his office. He agreed to see Rodgers at the Ammons' home at five thirty, together with his wife and son.

Rodgers arrived promptly. A maid showed him into the library where Ammons awaited him alone.

Ammons lifted a decanter. "Drink, Mr. Madden?"

"No, thanks." Rodgers tried to curb his impatience. "Are your wife and son at home, Mr. Ammons?"

"Yes. They'll be down shortly. I thought I might have a word with you first." His hand shook slightly and Rodgers felt a wave of compassion for him. He was still a young man but he was haggard, as though the trials of the past weeks had aged him prematurely. "Sit down, please, Mr. Madden."

Rodgers did so. Robert Ammons continued to stand, ill at ease, a man used to making decisions in the efficient management of his business, but a man out of his element in the present situation. Rodgers no longer felt impatient with him.

Ammons sighed. "I hardly know where to begin."

"Perhaps you could tell me a little about your son," Rodgers suggested. "There was very little information in the record. Is this the first time he has been in trouble?"

"It's his first arrest—yes. If that's what you mean." He smiled ruefully. "It's not the first time he's been drunk. Or even the first time he's been driving while drunk. He's been lucky not to have been caught before this."

"Or unlucky. This time he has seriously injured someone else."

"Yes. And it looks as if I'll be the one who has to pay for it. You bring them into the world and it's nothing but trouble from then on. Where's the joy parenthood's supposed to bring?"

"I take it you and your son aren't close."

"Close! Can anyone get close to this generation?" He sighed again. "I'm sorry. No need to take it out on you. We aren't close. I guess we never have been. Perhaps I'm more to blame than he is. My business really keeps me hopping and there just never seems to be enough time left over. I don't get to see much of the boy. I always intended to make it up to him—next summer, next year—I guess the years are going by rather quickly." He paused for a moment and stared hard at Rodgers. He said slowly, "You know, I think the last time I sat down and had a serious talk with him was when he was in the eighth grade. He wanted some pointers on football, and I used to be pretty good at it. Played in college, you know."

"Does your son play football now?"

"No. He didn't make the high school team. Must have been rather disappointing for him, too."

But he didn't know, Rodgers reflected. He hadn't taken time to find out.

"We've given him everything," said Ammons, suddenly petulant. "He's had a handsome allowance, his car since his sixteenth birthday, been allowed to come and go pretty much as he pleases. What makes a kid take advantage by going out and behaving so irresponsibly?"

"Perhaps to point up the fact that he is a kid," Rodgers said.

"I don't follow you."

"Maybe he wants you to crack down on him a little. Pay some attention to what he does."

"Well, I'm paying attention now! And I'll likely be paying a lot more than attention! This may even hurt my business. You'd be surprised."

72

"It could also hurt your son's future."

"He should have thought of that! But that's why I'm hiring you, to get him out of this mess. Kids'll sow their wild oats, I suppose, but he's got to learn something from this. I want you to talk to him."

Fred Ammons was a pimply-faced, surly boy. He slouched, managing to make expensively tailored slacks look ill fitted on him. He acknowledged the introduction to Rodgers with a curt nod and a dull "Hullo," his eyes never quite meeting Rodgers' gaze. Rodgers guessed he had had a. few drinks even then.

"Mr. Madden has a few questions he wants to ask you, Fred," explained Ammons.

"So? He's got questions, he can go to the library."

"Don't be rude," commanded his parent.

"So, who's being rude? Man, what's a library for? They got all those books, answer any question you want." He shrugged. "Okay, okay, so what you got to know? Am I innocent? Am I *ever* innocent."

"You're innocent of what?" queried Rodgers.

"Anything you got. You just name it, man, I'm innocent."

"Drunk driving?"

"Yeah."

"Hitting a pedestrian with your car?"

"Yeah. That, too. I wasn't even there."

"Won't hold up, Fred. Too many witnesses say you were there. You were drunk. You ran a man down."

Fred grimaced. "You got a real bad case of lying witnesses. You tell that to the judge. You tell him I said so. My word against theirs."

"It won't work, Fred. My advice is to plead guilty and throw yourself on the mercy of the court."

"Man, you got it all wrong! Ol' Fred here don't throw himself on nobody's mercy, especially not on some fuzz-lovin' judge."

"You won't get anywhere with this attitude," advised Rodgers. "You're going to have to show some signs of repentance."

"Repentance! What kind of talk is *that?* You sound like a priest."

"Never mind what *I* sound like. It's what *you* sound like we've got to change."

"What kind of crack's that?" demanded Fred.

"You sound like a first-class delinquent. You're begging to be incarcerated."

"Man, don't you know the *big* words!"

"I'm sure you know what I mean."

"If you think I'm going to the pen, you've lost your mind. Man, have you ever——"

"Pen?" whispered Ammons.

"Aw, he's just blowin' off to get a fat fee out of you, Dad."

"Shut up! *Is* there a possibility he could be sent to the penitentiary, Mr. Madden?"

"Well, I think the judge would certainly do that as a last resort. But if he shows no sign of realizing the seriousness of what he's done, and shows no remorse—it's a possibility."

"That would kill my wife. She's in bed over this as it is. I hope you won't need to talk to her."

"No, I see no reason to disturb her."

Fred grinned. "Poor Mother. This is going to hurt her more than it does me. You know, like they tell a kid about a spanking?"

Rodgers was depressed by the boy's callousness. He talked to him a few more minutes and left after advising him to think it over and come to his senses.

So, Green wasn't being bribed for this one. No judge, bribed or not, could excuse such flagrant disregard for the rights of others as Fred Ammons was exhibiting. Rodgers felt emotionally drained when he went home for his date with Alicia.

She met him at the door.

"You look beat. Want a drink—oh, I forgot. Sorry."

"I'm going to take a shower," he said. "I won't be long."

"Take your time. But don't forget I'm hungry."

Rodgers had put off talking to his great-grandmother; he couldn't delay indefinitely. He went up to her room half expecting she would already be asleep. She wasn't. She gave him a steady look with her old eyes that had seen so much of life—

the joy, sorrow, weakness, and strength of four generations of her family. Snapping off the reading light, she laid her Bible on the bedside table.

Rodgers sat down in the armchair near her bed, his head lowered dejectedly, and waited for the blow of her indignation to fall. When the silence remained unbroken, he glanced up to find her smiling.

"Has it been that bad, Rod?" she asked gently.

"It's been hard. I had to do it, Gran. I could see no way out. There *was* no way out."

"Then you did the right thing, if that's how you feel about it."

Relief washed over him. "I didn't expect you to take it this way."

"No. When you walked in here you looked as though you expected the guillotine."

"Well, I didn't expect you to agree with me."

"I don't agree with you. I think you are wrong. But I also believe you have done what you sincerely feel is right. For that I respect you. I suspect what happened was that you allowed yourself to be forced into a decision before you had prayed over it sufficiently. Am I correct?"

Rodgers got up restlessly. The respite from the guillotine had been brief.

"I prayed over it."

"All right. Perhaps I'm wrong. Perhaps this was His answer."

"I don't know. It seemed to be. Dad attempted suicide; I didn't see what else I could do."

"He's been very determined to have you in the firm."

"I've agreed to six months. That's all."

"Then you may return to the ministry?"

"I want to. Yes." He gazed fondly down at his great-grandmother. "Tell me, does life get any easier after ninety-one?"

She chuckled. "Who's ninety-one? Young man, don't you know better than to mention a lady's age to her? But to answer your question—it certainly gets no easier physically."

"Of course," he said compassionately. "But I really wasn't thinking of the physical."

She mused, "Sometimes I look into my mirror and I can't be-

75

lieve the old, old woman I see there is actually me." Her eyes shone into his. "You know, Rodgers, I'm very much younger inside. Deep inside. The part He feeds and cares for. The housing around me is about ready to scrap, I think. It's a miracle, isn't it, how temporary we are except for that one real part of us that is destined to live forever? We women waste so much time grooming and caring for the outside, and all our pains-taking efforts cannot make it endure long. We should spend our time on the soul that will live."

"You have spent your time on that," Rodgers said.

"Not enough. No one ever spends enough. My one regret is I've done so little for Him while He has done so much for me. You asked a question—it does get more tranquil as you near home, Rodgers. I feel at peace, only sometimes when I allow myself to fret, I fear the sickness or loneliness that may precede my death."

He bent swiftly and gathered her frail body close in his strong arms. "I'll be here. You won't be lonely, I promise you that."

For a moment the very old and the young, troubled each in their separate ways, clung to one another for comfort. Then his great-grandmother laughed and patted his shoulder. "We're being terribly sentimental! In another minute you'll have me in tears."

Rodgers stood. "An occasional cry is good for you. Too bad men can't use that release—be a lot less nervous disorders if we did, I suspect."

"I'll pray for you, Rodgers," Elizabeth Madden said. "I don't know whether your decision to join your father in the firm was right or wrong. But I shall pray for you."

"You might pray that I get back into the ministry after six months."

"I'll pray that you do His will," his great-grandmother corrected.

9

On Tuesday Rodgers gave himself the day off. Miss Hamilton would be busy adding the final touches to his office, a task she was all set to enjoy thoroughly. His father would be returning to the office the end of the week. Rodgers took what he supposed would be his last chance for a vacation before getting into the full swing of the firm's practice.

He found himself on the road to Hollis Creek, but he by-passed the small church. He drove instead to the Martin farm, hardly aware of his destination until he swung off the road at their gate. Mary Jane ran down the path to meet him.

"Well, you did come back!"

"I told you I would." He got out of the car.

"Pa's here. He's out back with a new calf. Do you want to meet him?"

Rodgers smiled down at the eager young girl—fresh and clean without make-up. "Your father or the calf?" he asked her.

She laughed. "My father, of course. The calf is a heifer." She grinned at him. "Or doesn't that tell you anything?"

Rodgers laughed. "Yes, I know what a heifer is. I'm probably a lot brighter than you think I am."

Her eyes flashed impishly. "I certainly hope so."

He allowed her to lead him around to a small pasture where a man in coveralls leaned on the gate.

Mary Jane called out to him. "Pa, this here's the young minister I was telling you about. Only he's a lawyer now."

Tom Martin turned and extended his hand. "Glad to meet

you, Mr. Madden." His steel blue eyes lowered slightly. "Sorry I wasn't home when you came to supper."

The man's handclasp was firm and warm. He had an open, honest face, though it was worn by anxious care.

"That's quite all right," Rodgers assured him.

"If you'd care to come again, I'll make it a point to be here," Martin said.

"I'll be glad to. Anytime."

"All right. Say, next Sunday?"

"Yes, that's fine. Thank you."

Rodgers was shown the new heifer, and then accompanied by both Martin and his daughter, he was given a tour of the farm. It brought in a living, though a somewhat meager one.

"We've had it a bit rough since my son joined up," Martin said. "Did Mary Jane tell you that Tommy's in Viet Nam?"

"I told him, Pa."

"Were you in the service, Mr. Madden?" Martin asked.

"Call me Rod, please, Mr. Martin," Rodgers requested.

"All right. And Tom here."

"Yes, I was in the service. Navy. It was before our involvement in Viet Nam."

"You aren't an objector to war, then?"

Rodgers smiled slowly. "Depends how you mean that. I don't like fighting or killing—but if you mean am I against serving my country, no, I'm not. I believe we must fight when we have to, to preserve the freedom we cherish."

"Yes. I feel that way, too. I don't believe in my boy gettin' killed though." His voice grew husky.

"No, and I don't blame you for that. It's the same for the other parents too, of course, and for the wives, sweethearts, and children of all our fighting men."

Martin smiled ruefully. "You're sayin' I'm not in it alone."

"You're not."

"I don't like the way we're fightin' this war, though," Martin said explosively. He threw a challenging glance at Rodgers. "I think we ought to blow 'em off the map and get it over. But I s'pose you wouldn't see it that way, would you?"

"There's no way to fight a war except to win," Rodgers replied.

"That's how I see it." Martin's eyes met Rodgers. "I ain't much for goin' to church. Especially now with Tommy away. I guess I sort of blame God for that, for the war and all."

"He's not to blame for it."

"I think sometime I'd like to have a talk with you, hear your views on God. Would you mind that?"

"No. I'd be glad to talk to you."

"Maybe Sunday night when you come. After supper."

"All right. Maybe I could help you out a bit around here until Tommy comes home," Rodgers offered.

"Oh, no, we couldn't think of askin' that. You have your hands full already, I'm sure."

"Not completely. The fresh air and sun will be good for me. The favor'd go both ways. You wouldn't be getting much. I don't know anything about farming."

"Nothing much to learn. Just hard work."

"It'd have to be late afternoon, except on Saturday."

"I sure can't afford to turn down free labor. Come whenever it suits you."

"You'll need work clothes," Mary Jane put in.

"I'll get some."

"There're some work pants and shirts of Tommy's here," Martin said, "but you're broader through the shoulders. A mite taller, too, I guess."

"Thanks, but it'll be no problem for me to pick up some jeans. I have plenty of old shirts."

Rodgers bid Martin good-by. Mary Jane accompanied him to his car.

"That was good of you to say you'll help us, Rod," she said.

"Not really. I'll be getting something from it."

"What?"

"You could have been my parishioners, if I'd been able to go to Hollis Creek. And I want to help your father."

"Do you think you can?"

"I hope so. I'll try. In a way I'll be fulfilling my ministry, so you see my motives aren't altogether altruistic."

"Altruistic? What's *that?*"

"Unselfish."

"Why didn't you say unselfish, then?"

"Because altruistic says the way I meant unselfish better."

She sighed. "I wish I knew more, like you do."

"I don't know so much. But you can learn by reading. I'll bring you some books. Will you read them?"

"Yes." She looked steadily into his eyes. "I'll read whatever you bring me."

"I'll bring them Sunday. Good-by, Mary Jane."

"You won't be back before Sunday?"

"Yes, I may."

He backed slowly to turn, thinking that she had an eager and probably intelligent mind. To him she was just a child; he could never be seriously interested in her romantically. He didn't want to become interested in any woman while his personal life was in such upheaval.

Rodgers passed the Hollis Creek Church, decelerating but not stopping. He couldn't pass it without emotion. He reflected grimly that he sorely needed to learn to take disappointment.

After dinner Rodgers went to his father's room. The elder Madden demanded to know straightway why he hadn't spent the day at the office.

"I saw no need to," Rodgers replied evenly. "It was being rearranged; I'd only have been in the way."

"How did you spend your time?"

"Drove out into the country."

Madden pursed his lips. "Hollis Creek, I suppose you mean."

"Not the church. I've met a family there—Martin. I went to see them."

"Why?"

"Why not?"

"If you want to visit, I know plenty of men it would help the firm for you to have lunch with."

"All right. On my own time, though, I will continue to see the Martins—and anyone else I want."

"Look here, Rod, we have to try to get along. You're giving me six months—do it cheerfully."

"I'm sorry. I'll try."

"Are you that unhappy?"

"No. It's just—a difficult adjustment."

Madden reached for a folded slip of paper on the bedside table and handed it to Rodgers. "Perhaps this will make the adjustment smoother."

Rodgers unfolded the check. It was for the amount of two hundred dollars.

"That's your salary for the week," Madden explained.

"Ten thousand, four hundred per year," said Rodgers.

"More than you'd have made at Hollis Creek, isn't it?"

"Considerably. Is it a bribe?"

"If you want to think of it that way. I hope it will induce you to stay on permanently."

"And if it doesn't you'll come up with something else."

"Not necessarily. I am trying to bring you to your senses. I'll admit that."

"And your needing me in the firm?"

"That was true. I do need you. Rod, a man wants to do everything he can for his son. I'd be less than human if I didn't feel that way about you."

"I've never accused you of being less than human."

"Somehow you make that sound like an insult."

"Perhaps."

Madden laughed. "Actually, you are a lot like me. You can be forced up to a point; after that you'll fight to have your own way. All right, Rod, take the rest of the week off. See these Martins if you want, make your adjustment. Monday morning report to me at the office ready to work. Do you think that's fair enough?"

"More than fair, yes."

"So do I. However, I would like to see you give your undivided attention to law."

"I'll earn my salary," Rodgers said crisply.

"Yes. I'll see that you do that much. And you can make it hard or pleasant between us. Your seminary training didn't come cheaply—how about showing me Christianity in action?"

"You might not like that; the firm could lose buisness. I think what you mean is that you want to see an example of the Christian son in action. Your idea of a Christian son."

"You may be right." Madden sighed. "I'm too tired to quibble with you over words tonight, Rod."

Rodgers stood. "I'll say good night. I am glad you're all right, Dad, and that you're home."

"Are you? I've wondered about that."

"I'm concerned about you. If I weren't, I'd hardly have given up so much for you."

Madden's lips tightened. "I'll try to see to it that you're repaid."

Rodgers smiled ruefully. "One or the other of us always has to give the conversation a bitter twist."

"So it seems. Perhaps that's the lawyer in us. You may find you're more of a lawyer than you realize."

Rodgers thought that over as he went out. Once he had felt his law training would be an invaluable aid to his ministry. Was it to be the other way round? Was he destined after all to have law as his career?

By the time Rodgers went to the Martins for dinner on Sunday evening, he had already seen a great deal of them during the week. Considerable repair had been made to the farm with his help—fences mended, the roof of the house fixed where shingles had blown off in spring storms, rotted boards replaced in the barn. He and Martin had worked companionably side by side, though they had talked very little.

After supper Mary Jane offered to help her mother in the kitchen, leaving the two men alone. Mr. Martin smiled at Rodgers. "Sit down, Rod. You and I have earned our rest this Sabbath."

Rodgers grinned and studied his hands with their new callouses. "I guess we have at that."

"Won't be the same without you. I guess you go into law practice tomorrow, don't you?"

"Yes, but I'll be around here occasionally."

"Rod, I don't mean to pry," Martin said, leaning forward in his chair, "but how come you left the ministry for law?"

Rodgers explained briefly, omitting the precise legal ramifications, stating only that his father had been ill and needed him.

Martin nodded. "I understand from Mary Jane that you didn't really want to go into law."

"No, I didn't."

"Well, I admire you for helping your father. I'm sure he appreciates it." This was a father's answer, from one who was sorely longing for the help of his own son. It was not at all the way Wickham saw it. Rodgers found himself wishing pointlessly that the two men were more of the same mind, or rather that Wickham shared Martin's point of view. But he didn't. For Wickham, a commitment to the Lord Jesus Christ pushed aside all other considerations in life and all other commitments. And that was the way it should be, viewed from its simplest standpoint, thought Rodgers; only life could seldom be viewed from the simplest standpoint. Relationships with people complicated the picture. He had decided the matter in his own heart and soul— why then did it not stay settled and give him some measure of peace?

None of the inner turmoil he felt showed in Rodgers' face as he talked to Martin. This was a man who needed help and he had set himself the task of providing it.

"Would you like to talk about your son?" Rodgers asked gently.

The older man sighed and his face grew somber. "I'm not sure. Yes, I guess it might help to talk." He smiled. "Anyway it's what I've planned all week to do with this evening. Only now you're here, I can't seem to begin."

Rodgers leaned back in his chair, relaxed and waiting. He made no effort to prompt the other man. Speech would come. Emotion had been bottled up in Martin for too long; he wanted relief.

"When I go over it in my mind," Martin said finally, "I know it's no more unfair for my son to go to war than for anyone else's. A war comes, we have to fight. I understand that. I even accept it. And this was Tommy's turn. I understand that, too. Do you see?"

Rodgers nodded and did not speak.

"But understanding is not feeling. In my mind I understand, but in my heart——" Martin looked down at his hands which were clasped loosely between his knees. "Inside it's like I was flying apart." He glanced up. "I drink. I don't know if you've known that?"

Rodgers nodded again without comment.

"It helps sometimes. Oh, I know it's the wrong thing to do. But sometimes I have to forget. Maybe you can't understand that."

"Yes, I understand."

"So, what's the answer? I suppose you've got one."

"Only the obvious. Turn to God. Don't try to carry the burden of your worry alone."

"Ah, yes. But I guess I blame Him for all this. He is all powerful—you do believe *that,* don't you?"

"Yes, I certainly do."

"Then He could stop the war and bring peace to the world."

"In a way, that's true. But only in a way."

"What do you mean?"

"We ourselves are blocking peace. We have brought about our own wars—the human race has. God has given us free will and with that free will most men have chosen to reject their Creator. Now, God could bring about peace by overriding our free will. But He doesn't."

"Why?"

"I don't know. Perhaps because He wants men, not puppets. He wants us to come to Him of our own free will. Society can be changed only as individual men are changed. Reform begins within a single human heart."

Martin smiled slightly. "I suppose I shouldn't have expected any other answer from a preacher. But if I lose Tommy?"

"God gave *His* only Son for you, Tom. If you lose Tommy, you will not be without hope. We know that the dead who are in Christ have only passed from life to Life. We have the hope of resurrection to a life that lasts for all eternity."

"You really believe that, do you?"

"Yes. It's true. You have a Bible, haven't you?"

"It's here somewhere."

"I'll give you something to read." Rodgers took out paper and pencil and scribbled a brief notation. He handed it to Martin. "Read this passage before you go to bed tonight. Think about it. I'll give you more next time I come."

Martin looked at the paper. "I Corinthians 15:12-58."

"Paul's letter to the church at Corinth. Written by the inspiration of the Holy Spirit, so it's God's word to you."

Martin put the paper into his pocket. "All right, I'll read it. I promise you that. We'll see if it helps."

"God will do His part," said Rodgers. "See that you do yours."

10

The summer passed, and fall came. Rodgers worked hard in the law firm and continued to maintain his friendship with the Martin family. He attended church with his parents, somehow unable to attend at Hollis Creek where he had longed to minister. He steadfastly refused Broyles' invitation to teach a Sunday school class, and he avoided any contact with Wilbur Wickham.

Then, unexpectedly, he was thrown with the elderly minister one Sunday evening in October. Rodgers arrived at the Martin home, where he had been invited to dinner, to find Wickham a guest also. Covering momentary embarrassment, Rodgers extended his hand to Wickham.

"Hello, Wilbur, it's good to see you again."

"Is it?" asked Wickham astutely.

Rodgers laughed, surprised. "All right. I wasn't particularly glad to see you when I came in, but I am now."

Wickham said, "Good. I'm glad to see you, too, but then I knew you were going to be here when I accepted their invitation."

"There's no reason for us to avoid each other," Rodgers replied.

"I haven't avoided you."

"All right! There's no reason for *me* to avoid *you*, then."

"There's no reason for you to be upset, either," said Wickham.

They entered the sitting room and Tom said expansively, "Sit down! Everyone, sit down, please!" Mary Jane smiled as though concealing a choice secret with great difficulty. Eva Martin bustled out toward the kitchen, her cheeks flushed with excitement. What was going on, wondered Rodgers, realizing suddenly that the air was electric with expectancy. Eva Martin returned bearing a tray of amber colored drinks.

"Ah, here we are!" said Martin. "We have news that requires a toast." He glanced with a smile at Rodgers. "As my dear friend here has helped free me from dependence on alcohol, this is pure apple juice." He chuckled. "Not even *hard* cider, Rod."

Rodgers laughed and accepted a glass. "What's your big news?"

"Just a minute now till we're all served." Martin watched as Mary Jane helped her mother pass the tray. Then he lifted his own glass. "Our Tommy is on his way home from Viet Nam, safe and sound. His tour is over. We heard this morning."

"Say, that's great news!" Rodgers exclaimed. "I'm very happy for you."

"It seems like a miracle," said Eva Martin. "We've been so worried."

"I was beside myself," Martin confessed, "as you all know. Rod here helped me get straight. Wilbur, I don't believe you know all he's done for me, do you?"

Wickham smiled. "You've told me some of it. I'd like to hear the rest."

Then Martin was off. Throughout dinner Rodgers was forced to listen as his virtues were extolled. When Martin paused for breath, Wickham urged him to go on.

Finally Rodgers protested. "Can't we change the subject? I hate to be discussed while I'm present."

Wickham laughed. "Sorry. We didn't realize it was bothering you."

"Of course it is. I don't deserve such praise."

"You're too modest," said Martin. "If I'd done for anyone what you've done for me, I'd be bragging."

"If you think I've helped you, I'm glad," Rodgers replied, "but the credit really goes to God. Of course, you really helped yourself, too."

"Well, I won't argue with you. Perhaps we should change the subject."

And they did, for Rodgers' sake. But he remained quiet, almost aloof. Wickham glanced thoughtfully at him from time to time.

It was still early in the evening when Wickham rose to leave. "I really must be getting home. Tom picked me up, Rod, but if you could drop me off, it'd save him a trip out."

"Sure. Be glad to."

Good nights were said, and then Rodgers was alone with Wickham in the car. He was silent on the drive to the manse, more tense than he'd been at the Martins'. When they were almost there Wickham broke the silence.

"You aren't happy, are you, Rod?"

"No, I'm not happy. Far from it."

Wickham nodded. "I see quite a change in you. The light's gone from your eyes. You've lost weight. What's worrying you, Rod?"

"Nothing. I'm not worried." He sighed. "I'm just tired, I guess, Wilbur. Dog tired. And—more or less discouraged."

"Why? You did a remarkable job on Tom Martin. I know what he was like when his boy left. I tried to reach him myself and got nowhere at all with him. God was able to use you to help that man."

Rodgers was silent.

"You're too modest, but if you don't want to talk about it, we won't I would like to help you, though."

"Thanks, Wilbur, but I'm not sure you can."

"What's happening to you? Are you violating your conscience by the things you're doing in your law practice?"

Rodgers snorted. "Where'd you get an idea like that?"

"Never mind. Are you?"

"No. I've done nothing wrong."

"Well, something's bothering you."

"I just haven't been able to accept my disappointment. I haven't been able to shake the depression that's gripped me." He looked quickly at Wickham. "I know you think I made the wrong decision. Don't tell me that again."

"Yes, I think it's obvious you did. But what's bothering you now goes deeper than that. I was afraid it would."

Rodgers gave a short laugh. "You've been reading too much psychological hogwash."

"You feel rejected," Wickham ventured. "You should know better, Rod, but you're not using your head. You're letting your emotions distort your judgment."

"That's utter nonsense!"

"You chose to leave, you know. He didn't cast you out. He doesn't revoke a pastoral call."

"Yes. You said that before."

"It bears repeating; you didn't listen before. If you were doing His will, you would be happy about it."

Rodgers stopped the car in the manse driveway. He glanced at Wickham.

"Well, that's true, isn't it?" argued the old minister. "When we walk according to His way, it brings peace, does it not?"

"Yes, I've always believed that."

"And do you have peace now?"

"You know I don't."

"Well, then?"

"It's not that simple."

"Isn't it? Do you honestly believe you are walking in His way?"

"Perhaps this *is* His way. Maybe the trouble is that I'm not accepting it. Could it be that God is trying to teach me something or direct me in a certain way through these circumstances? It's just that I have to get to the point where I can accept this delay as God's will."

"I don't agree, but I see I can never change your mind." Wickham touched the door handle. "I always have hot milk before I go to bed. Want some?"

"If I were wise, I'd turn you down."

"We've already established that you are not wise."

Rodgers laughed. "Flattery's not your long suit."

"You don't need flattery." Wickham smiled. "At least your sense of humor is returning, if not your good judgment."

"No one's ever denied that you are good for the soul, my dear friend."

"So, I'm reinstated as the good friend."

"I've never thought otherwise of you, Wilbur."

Wickham patted his arm. "Come in and we'll have that hot milk."

They had hot cocoa before a cheerful fire. Rodgers sighed. "This is real comfort."

"Make yourself at home."

"I have." He frowned, for a moment remembering this was to have been his home. Then the pain passed. The two men sat for a long while in companionable silence—watching the flickering firelight, dreaming, sipping the hot chocolate.

Finally Wickham said, "You've relaxed. Can we talk?"

"And wind me up again?" Rodgers stretched and sat up. "All right, Wilbur, go ahead. What else do you want to say?"

"First—you really did a marvelous job on Martin, as I've told you."

"Yes. As everyone has told me. I'm thoroughly convinced of it myself now—so what else?"

"Do you agree it took faith on your part to inspire it in someone else?"

"Of course."

"And yet I feel you are resentful toward God because you consider—probably not consciously—that He has rejected you. Now, don't protest," Wickham said as Rodgers lifted his hands. "I want you to think about it, as a possibility."

"All right, I wanted to be a minister. I'm a lawyer."

"You see? You are resentful."

"I haven't understood. I suppose I'd have to agree with that. I don't think I *blame* Him, I just feel hurt."

"I know you do. But use your head, Rod. Why would God revoke your call?"

"He wanted a lawyer instead of a minister."

"No. In that case you would have adjusted better."

"That's my fault. I've never said my unhappiness was not my own fault."

"I think it is your fault but not because you haven't adjusted. You're unhappy because you are out of His will for your life and following your own design. That's why it's so hard for you."

Rodgers shook his head. "I still don't agree with you." He looked at his watch. "I'd better go, it's getting late."

90

"All right." Wickham stood with him. "Forgive me for preaching to you, Rod, and for judging you, too. I hope you'll come back."

Rodgers grinned. "And next time you won't preach?"

Wickham smiled. "I don't promise that. I'll probably keep after you until I get you back where you belong."

They shook hands affectionately and Rodgers left. He drove home slowly. He had much to think over. However, no amount of thinking altered his conviction that he had made the only decision possible regarding his father. He still saw it as his duty to help him. The attempted suicide could hardly be shrugged off. Perhaps sometime he could return to the ministry; that hope was uppermost in his heart, but there was an ever greater despair and a presentiment that he would not. Wickham had said he was afraid God would not lead him back to the ministry; about his fear at least Wickham was likely correct.

"You're late," his father greeted him crossly from the open library door.

Rodgers walked into the library. "A little."

"Where've you been? Must you spend every Sunday evening with those hick friends of yours?"

Rodgers' lips tightened. He didn't reply, however.

"Were you there all this time?" Madden pressed.

"No. I've been with Wickham."

"The Hollis Creek minister?"

"That's right."

"I didn't know you were still seeing him."

"What is it? Was there something you wanted me for this evening?"

"Yes. I wanted to take a client to the club for dinner. I did take him, in fact. I wanted you along."

"I'm sorry. You didn't tell me."

Madden relaxed with a smile. Rodgers was after all being quite amiable. "It doesn't matter. You can go next time. I should have made my plans sooner."

"Is this client important to you?"

"Not particularly. They are all important. He has a good case and he can pay for our services."

"What sort of service does he require?"

"He's charged with income tax evasion."

"Uh-oh. Guilty?"

"Our job is to prove he's not. He has a secretary who was keeping the books. She's left town. It'll be your job to try to locate her. I have some leads you can run down."

"Okay. I'll get on it in the morning."

"Rod?"

"Yes?"

"Don't get too involved with this Wickham, will you? You're just beginning to shape up."

"You'll get your six months. We didn't bargain for more than that," Rodgers said crisply.

"Wickham wasn't in the bargain."

"There was no bargain concerning Wickham. I've lived up to my part. Don't expect too much Dad."

Madden gave in. He knew when to press and when to let up. Pushed into a corner, Rodgers would fight.

"You're almost rid of Green," Rodgers said. "By Christmas he'll be off your back entirely. I've less than half a dozen cases to finish up."

"I know. And I appreciate it. You've done a good job. Particularly on the Ammons case, getting probation for young Fred. I know that wasn't easy under the circumstances."

"If the man he hit hadn't recovered, I couldn't have managed it."

"Well, you have done a good job. I want you to know I appreciate all the hard work you've put in."

"You do intend to keep it clean? I won't bail you out a second time."

"You won't have to."

"Just so we understand each other," said Rodgers.

"I've always understood you," his father replied.

"What's the name on this tax evasion case?"

"Brewster. John Brewster. The secretary's name is Madelyn

Wythe. She's supposed to have some relatives in Chicago—an aunt, I think. You might want to start there."

"And you think this Madelyn Wythe altered the books?"

"That's what Brewster claims. She stole money that was supposed to go for the taxes and then fixed the books to try to show less tax was owed."

"Do you believe him? That he had nothing to do with it?"

"Yes. I think he's too smart to think he could get away with a thing like that. The government checks pretty close, you know."

"How do they feel about this secretary angle?"

"Oh, I think they're keeping an open mind—but not too open. They're inclined to doubt his story."

"Are they looking for Madelyn Wythe?"

"Yes. Probably not too hard. Anyway, I'd like to find her first."

"Why?"

"Now you've been a lawyer long enough to know the answer to that. I don't like surprises."

"You think her story will differ from Brewster's?"

"Sure. If you were in her place, wouldn't yours?"

"I guess so."

"You know it. Of course she'll deny any involvement."

"Then it'll be her word against his."

"We may find proof he's right."

"Or that *she* is."

Madden smiled. "Brewster is our client. Keep that in mind."

"You aren't suggesting you'd fake the evidence?"

"No. But I'm not saying I'd present evidence harmful to him either."

"That's a thin, gray line!"

"Perhaps. A lawyer has to walk a thin line, and if you want to call it gray, I suppose sometimes it is."

"I won't do anything that goes against my conscience, good law or not," Rodgers said. "You'd better keep *that* in mind."

"Just find the girl for me. That's all I've asked you to do. I'll take care of everything else."

Rodgers searched his father's eyes uneasily. "If I ever find out you aren't leveling with me——"

Madden grinned and clapped him firmly on the shoulder. "Don't worry so much! I've told you over and over everything's all right. How many times do you want to hear it?"

Rodgers shook his head. "I've heard it enough, I suppose."

"But you don't quite trust me. I can't help that, can I?" After a moment, Madden said, "Now, let me put you on the witness stand. There's something your mother's been after me to talk to you about. I suppose tonight is as good a time as any."

"Oh? What?"

"This family you see so much of—the Martins. There's a girl, isn't there?"

Rodgers smiled. "They have a daughter, yes."

"Do you care a great deal for her?"

"I'm fond of her, yes."

"In love with her?"

"No. She's just a good friend."

"But you spend a lot of time there."

"Not solely because of the girl. I like the whole family. The son is due back from Viet Nam soon and his absence has been a hardship for them. I've tried to help out."

"Oh, I see. Well, your mother was worried. She thought you might be planning to marry the girl."

"I'm not planning to marry anyone just yet."

Madden smiled a bit self-consciously. "Well, you know how mothers are. She wants you to stay in your own class."

"And what class is that?" Rodgers asked innocuously.

"Oh no, you don't. You aren't dragging me into that kind of argument."

"The Martins are good, decent people. Mary Jane hasn't had many advantages, but if I loved her that wouldn't stop me from marrying her. However, I'm not in love, so you can tell Mother to relax."

Madden stood up. "I will. And in the morning, we'll arrange your trip to Chicago. I'd like for you to leave as soon as possible."

11

Rodgers left for Chicago the following afternoon. He arrived at O'Hare airport and took the airport limousine into the Loop, getting out at the Palmer House. After dinner he made preliminary telephone calls to a number of hotels before retiring for the night. He did not locate Madelyn Wythe in this initial effort.

The following day he took a cab out to Elmhurst where her aunt lived. Mrs. Marvin Lawson resided alone in a modestly furnished home left to her by her late husband. She hadn't heard from her niece in several months.

"Is she in some sort of trouble, Mr. Madden?"

"Not that we know of. We just need to locate her. Did you know she was employed by John Brewster?"

Mrs. Lawson folded her hands in her lap and met his eyes candidly. "Yes, she's mentioned him in her letters. I believe she was well satisfied with her work. She spoke well of Mr. Brewster."

"Did you think it unusual not to hear from her?"

"No, not particularly. We didn't correspond regularly or frequently."

"Then you made no effort to contact her?"

"I wrote to her but I wasn't concerned when she didn't answer. I assumed she was just busy about her own affairs." She smiled at him. She was a pretty woman in her mid-forties, with brown hair beginning to streak with gray. "After all, young girls don't always have the time to correspond, you know."

Rodgers smiled. "How old is she?"

"Twenty-three."

"She's worked for Mr. Brewster two years, I believe."

"Yes. She started soon after she got out of business college. She was pleased with her position with Mr. Brewster. She said it paid well." She frowned. "You say she has left there? I can't understand why she would do that." She looked at Rodgers. "Why are you looking for Madelyn?"

"My father and I are representing Mr. Brewster. Madelyn is needed as a witness."

"For Mr. Brewster?"

"Well—for the truth. We just want to get the truth."

"Is Mr. Brewster in some kind of trouble?"

"Yes. He's accused of income tax evasion."

"Oh! Oh, my goodness. Well, Mr. Madden, I can tell you that Madelyn wouldn't be mixed up in anything wrong. She's a good girl, an honest, decent girl."

"But it looks bad for her, running away. If she has done nothing wrong, she has nothing to be afraid of. If you know where she is——"

"No, I don't. Really, Mr. Madden, I'm not keeping anything from you."

"I hope not. I have no desire to hurt your niece, Mrs. Lawson."

"Do you know what Madelyn looks like? Have you seen her?"

"I have a picture, but I have never seen her in person."

"Would it help you to see some other snapshots of her?"

"Yes. Different angles and views sometimes alter the appearance."

She left the room for a few minutes and came back with a small album.

"These are pictures my sister sent me of Madelyn, taken over the years, and some later ones from Madelyn herself."

"Is your sister still living?"

"No. I'm Madelyn's only living relative."

Rodgers looked through the album, turning quickly past the baby and childhood pictures until he reached some taken in her late teens and early twenties. She was a pretty girl with honey blond hair that had turned to a golden brown in the recent pictures. Color snaps showed deep blue eyes and even white teeth. Her complexion was fair and clear; the warm eyes looked at him candidly with a touch of humor sparkling in their depths. He paused longest over a color photograph taken nearly full face.

"I believe that's your favorite," said Mrs. Lawson.

"It's a lovely picture."

"It's a very good likeness of Madelyn. It was taken last spring. Would you like to take that one with you?"

"If you don't object."

"I have a larger copy. Here, let me slip it out for you."

She took it from the album and gave it to Rodgers. He put it in a clean envelope and slid it into his breast pocket.

"I'll see that you get this back when I'm through with it."

"Don't worry about that."

Rodgers closed the album. "I won't take up any more of your time. If you should hear from your niece, I'd appreciate a call. I'll be staying at the Palmer House."

She saw him to the door, smiling pleasantly. "I will call you if I hear from her. But if she's running away, I don't suppose she will contact me. I can't think what would possess her to behave this way. Madelyn is a Christian girl."

Rodgers smiled. "That's good to know. I hope I can find her so we can clear all of this up. Good-by, and thank you for your cooperation."

Where should he look next, he wondered. He went to the hotel and put in a call to his father.

"Stay in Chicago a while longer," Madden said. "Show the picture at hotels and rooming houses. She may be using another name. Check banks and charge accounts. She withdrew several hundred dollars before she left here. She may be employed, or seeking employment."

"I'm not a detective, you know," Rodgers complained.

"You'll learn. It's just leg work and asking questions. Good luck. And you might move into a cheaper place since you'll be there awhile."

"Okay. I'll try to get a room at the Y. I'll let you know."

Rodgers found a room at the Y.M.C.A. downtown, then checked out of the Palmer House. When he notified Mrs. Lawson of his change of address, she told him there had been no word yet from Madelyn, but she promised to let him know.

Before he went to bed that night, he took out the picture Mrs. Lawson had given him of Madelyn and stared at it for a long time, memorizing each feature and flicker of expression. The girl seemed about to speak, so eloquent were her radiant eyes and expressive mouth.

He took the pictures with him as he traveled about Chicago, showing them to hotel clerks, rooming house landladies, apartment superintendents. He took them into offices, stores, banks, employment bureaus. He tried hospitals and police—all without success or a single lead.

Two days before Thanksgiving his father telephoned. "No leads yet, Rodgers?"

"None. I don't see much point in continuing here."

"Well, come home for the holidays, at least. We'll try to figure out what to do next."

"I'll talk to the aunt one more time and then I'll be home."

Mrs. Lawson seemed glad to see him. Her living room was warm with a cheery fire.

"Come in, Mr. Madden," she invited. "My, you must be nearly frozen. I believe we'll have some snow, don't you?"

"I shouldn't be at all surprised. This is a pleasant fire."

"Would you care for coffee? It's already made; I was going to have some myself."

"I would indeed." He sat down in the cozy room and relaxed. Taking out Madelyn Wythe's picture, he gazed at it by flickering firelight. The lighting was just right for the girl. Her eyes came alive, highlights danced in her golden hair. The picture held a strange attraction for him.

He chuckled at himself. *All you need to do, Rod, is fall in love with a girl you don't even know, a girl who quite likely has stolen money and committed a crime against the federal government for which she may have to spend several years in prison.*

But he didn't really believe that. Since first seeing the black and white photo of her in his father's office, he had not believed it. And now sitting in her aunt's parlor, looking at the color photo by firelight, he knew he must find her some way and prove her innocence.

Mrs. Lawson was returning down the hall. Rodgers slipped the plastic covered picture into his pocket.

"I take it you haven't found Madelyn," Mrs. Lawson said as she poured his coffee.

He took the cup, added sugar and cream. "No. No trace of her. I'm convinced she's not in Chicago. You haven't heard?"

"Not a word. Frankly, I'm a little uneasy. Do you think something might have happened to her?"

Rodgers shook his head. "In that case, you would have been notified. She wanted to disappear, I think, and she has. That's why she hasn't contacted you. Christmas is coming; perhaps you'll have some word then."

"Yes. She usually comes here for Christmas."

"Well, I doubt that she'll come, but she may contact you."

"You really don't believe anything has happened to her?"

"No, I don't." The expectancy in his heart was too strong; the girl was alive.

"Perhaps there's something that I should tell you, Mr. Madden. It didn't seem to mean very much before, but now——"

He sat forward, his interest aroused. "What is it?"

"A few years ago Madelyn was in New Orleans with her parents. She was completely taken with that old city, particularly with the Vieux Carré."

"You think she may have gone to New Orleans?"

"It's possible, I'd say. If she did, she would be in the French Quarter. I'm sure of that."

"I suppose it's worth a try. I may check there." He spoke casually, though he'd move heaven and earth now to go to New Orleans. But it was important for his personal interest in the girl to remain secret. Too personal an involvement in her cause could motivate his father to remove him from the case.

"I hope you will. I am worried about Madelyn."

"Don't worry." He smiled reassuringly. "I'll see you get her back safe and sound. That's a promise."

She returned his smile. "I don't know how you are going to do it, but I trust you."

Rodgers spent Thanksgiving with his family. He told his father of the clue connecting Madelyn Wythe to New Orleans and Madden was all for his going there. The trip was arranged for the following Monday. In the meantime Rodgers had a chance to see the Martins and Wilbur Wickham.

Tommy Martin was home, the family was united and happy, the farm was doing well, and Tom Martin himself was a changed man from the defeated person Rodgers had first met. He had regained his self-respect and confidence. Rodgers had a good visit with them, and then Mary Jane walked out to his car with him. Her eager young face barely concealed suppressed excitement.

Rodgers smiled down at her. "Well, what's *your* big news?"

She laughed. "You can tell it's something, huh?"

"I surely can. You're quite transparent."

Her face clouded for a moment. "Is that good?"

He grinned. "Yes, that's good. Don't keep me in suspense now. What is it?"

"I'm goin' to take a business course! With Tommy home, I can be spared from some of the chores. I'll still be here to help Ma out in the evenin's. But, Rod, I'm goin' to take this course and then I can get a real good job. What do you think of that?"

"I'm very proud of you. I know you'll do well."

She thanked him almost shyly and stepped back. "Well, I just wanted you to know. You've helped us all so much, Rod. There's no way to thank you."

It was his turn to be uncomfortable. He got into the car. "There's no need to thank me." He was surprised to hear Mary Jane laugh. "Now what is it?" he asked roughly.

"You." She looked at him indulgently. "You have a problem, do you know that? You can't take praise."

"Don't be silly," he said.

"It's true. You can't." She laughed again and waved. " 'By, Rod. Have fun in New Orleans."

Rodgers found his old friend Wilbur Wickham ill with a deep chest cold. The elderly minister was up, sitting in his den reading, but it was evident he didn't feel well.

"You'd better take care of that cough," Rodgers warned.

"Oh, I'll be all right. I've had coughs before. How's the law?"

"I'm working on a case that will take me to New Orleans for a while."

"You'll be back by Christmas, won't you?"

"Oh, yes, I expect to."

"And are you still planning to leave the firm in January?"

"Yes."

"Perhaps you'll get to Hollis Creek after all. This detour may not have hurt you as much as I feared it would."

"Well, we'll see."

Wickham searched the younger man's eyes. "You don't seem as unhappy as you were."

Rodgers was frank. "No. But I've lost the joy I once had. It's as though a fire has burned out in me."

"You will have to come back into a close fellowship with Him to get it rekindled."

"And how do I do that?"

"If you really don't know, how can I help you?" Wickham asked.

Rodgers sighed. "I seem unable to help myself."

"You know how to start. You can't have forgotten that."

"I know what I would advise anyone else. Somehow it doesn't seem to work for me. I get up in the morning, I go through the motions of living, and then at night I go to bed. There's no meaning to it, and no joy. Inside, I feel completely dead."

"Of course. Life is empty without Christ. The trouble is, Rod, you are still blaming God for everything that's gone wrong for you."

Rodgers grinned wryly. "Now let's *not* go over all *that* again."

"Sorry."

"Actually, I'm not as unhappy as I was. I suppose I'm beginning to make some sort of adjustment."

"To what? You can go on without Him, is that it?"

"Now you said that, I didn't." Rodgers got up restlessly. "I'll be all right, Wilbur. I'll work it out. Anyway, I didn't come here to worry you. Take care of that cold, do you hear?"

"Sure, don't worry about my cold. Take care of yourself and don't stay away too long."

Rodgers spent some time with Alicia. She was happy and seemed to be making real headway as a witnessing Christian. She even had some of her old friends taking a renewed interest in the church.

"And you, Rod?" she asked. "Are you getting along all right?"

"Sure. I'm fine."

"Who is this girl you are looking for?"

Rodgers took out the color photo of Madelyn Wythe and showed it to her.

"Wow! She's a real doll, isn't she!"

"Oh, she's pretty enough, I guess."

"And she's a criminal?"

"No. I didn't say she was a criminal. We just want to question her."

"What about?" She grinned up at him. "*I* would want to question her, if I were *you*."

"About her former employer," Rodgers said.

"Oh, yeah? Is that all?"

He smiled. "What else did you expect?"

"Well, an attractive girl like that, I'd hope you might want to ask her for a date. It's time you thought about settling down, brother dear."

"Time enough for that. And I haven't even met this girl yet."

"You'll find her, and when you do, keep what I said in mind."

Later, in his own room with the picture of Madelyn Wythe propped up on the bureau where he could see it easily, Rodgers was thoughtful. So Alicia approved of the girl. What was there about the lively, smiling face that appealed to both of them? Was it only excellent photography, or was there a strength of personality so powerful that the camera had captured it almost intact on celluloid? He was anxious to get to New Orleans and search for her. It did not occur to him for a moment to wonder if he would be disappointed in Madelyn Wythe; he looked forward to meeting the girl whose picture he had carried about with him for so long.

12

Rodgers arrived in New Orleans on Monday. He had been unable to reach Wilbur Wickham before he left and had asked his father to call and let him know that he would be staying at the Monteleone in the French Quarter.

Rodgers had been to New Orleans twice before. The old picturesque city, particularly the Vieux Carré, fascinated him. Initially, he spent several days walking the streets, intrigued by ancient buildings reminiscent of a bygone era of Southern history. Rodgers could tell himself that these structures were musty, crumbling, and probably rat infested, but he could not dispel the mood of the French Quarter or escape its enchantment.

Everywhere he went, Rodgers showed his pictures of Madelyn Wythe. One afternoon he stopped in a pastry shop on Royal Street for coffee and a sandwich. When the waitress brought his check, he showed her the pictures. She studied them with interest.

"Yes, I've seen this girl."

"You're sure?" Rodgers asked.

"Oh, yes. I wouldn't easily forget a face like that. Actually, your pictures don't do her justice—there's a radiance to her face that seems to come from within, like light glowing through the translucent shade of a lamp. Do you know what I mean?" She lifted her brows and shrugged. "I'm an artist; maybe you don't understand what I'm saying. But I have seen her before—that's what you wanted to know."

"Where?"

"In here. For coffee."

"When?"

She shrugged again. "I can't say. I may have seen her on the street, too. She frequents the French Quarter, I believe."

So, he was getting warmer at last. It was like the game he'd played as a kid — you are cold, warm, now you're getting hot. He would make no inquiries from here on. It would be better to find her himself on the street or in some little shop than run the risk of scaring her off.

The next few days he spent in the Vieux Carré, visiting little shops, eating at unique restaurants, always searching for the girl. The delightful weather held—mild, sunny, typical of New Orleans. Rodgers visited the wharf, watching huge cargo ships dock. He crossed on the ferry. He toured the museums. Occasionally he went inside the historic old Saint Louis Cathedral, but it was not spiritually satisfying; it had become too much a museum itself.

On a rainy afternoon in mid-December Rodgers caught his first glimpse of the girl. He had tired of touring the damp little shops in search of her and had gone inside the Saint Louis Cathedral to rest. Lost in thought amidst the statues and flickering prayer candles, he was disturbed by the entrance of a tour group. With a sigh of irritation he turned around in the pew and found himself staring directly into the eyes of the young woman seated a few rows behind him. She smiled in sympathy with his annoyance, a dazzling and sweet smile. Her face was framed by a snowy mantilla of delicate lace through which he could see the brown-gold of her hair. Rodgers caught his breath with an audible gasp and the girl smiled at him again, then got up and slipped out past the tourists.

Before Rodgers could untangle his feet and follow, she was out of the church. He hurried outside to the street where he stood bare-headed in the drizzle, searching for her. He caught sight of the white mantilla again in Jackson Square and raced across the street. An oncoming car swerved to avoid hitting him and honked a protest. Rodgers ran on, into the park. The flash of white appeared briefly at the west side gate. He dashed for it in time to see the girl enter the Pontalba apartment buildings opposite.

He did not search for her there; alerted, she might flee the city. He would have to continue as he had before and hope to run into her again. In the future he would stay closer to the cathedral and Jackson Square. How he would approach her when he did find her again was a problem he didn't consider now.

Rodgers next saw the girl on a Monday morning at the French Market Cafe Monde near the wharf, where he was accustomed to taking his morning coffee. She glanced at him briefly, then looked away. She was conservatively dressed, as though on her way to work, he thought. He watched her covertly but made no effort to approach her. He had decided that when he did finally speak to her, it must appear to be an outgrowth of numerous chance meetings. He had rejected the simpler approach of handing her a summons to appear as a witness in court. He realized that he was making this decision for purely personal reasons; there was no real point in delaying telling her of her involvement in the case against her employer, or of the use the defense intended to make of her disappearance. He did not want to believe she was involved; that was his main problem. What bothered him particularly was the fact that she had run away. He didn't believe she was guilty, and yet she had run. Why?

Rodgers wished he weren't getting so personally involved. The interest he had felt after seeing her picture had exploded into a deeper, more permanent emotion on seeing the girl herself. He sat in the early morning sunlight, his eyes half closed, and listened as she talked to the waiter. He couldn't catch her words, only the soothing tone of her voice and the lilting note of happiness in it.

She left presently and Rodgers watched as she cut through Jackson Square. He guessed from the hour of her morning coffee that she worked somewhere nearby. He remained at the coffee stand for a few more minutes, then walked through the square himself and over to Canal Street. He wanted to pick out a few Christmas presents to mail home. By chance he found Madelyn Wythe's place of employment. She was a clerk behind the lingerie counter in Holmes Department Store. When Rodgers approached her, she looked up with a courteous smile.

"May I help you, sir?"

"Yes. I'm looking for a gift for my sister."

"What did you have in mind? A slip, or a gown?"

"A slip, I guess. Something white and frilly."

"Do you know her size?"

"She's five-five, slender. Can you tell from that?"

She smiled. "I think so."

She showed him several styles and he selected one and gave her the mailing address. He watched closely; she gave no sign of recognizing the city. As he paid her, she asked casually, "You aren't from New Orleans, then?"

"No. I've been here for several weeks."

"On vacation?" Her tone was conversational, but her eyes avoided direct contact with his own.

"Not altogether. I have some business here."

She smiled and handed him his receipt, saying briskly, "I hope your sister enjoys the slip, sir. It's been a pleasure to serve you. Come again."

The following morning she spoke to him at the coffee stand.

"Good morning, Mr. Madden."

Pleasantly surprised, he returned her greeting and asked permission to join her. It was granted.

"You're one up on me," he said when he was seated opposite her. "I don't know *your* name."

Her eyes met his candidly. "Don't you?" she asked. Before he could reply, she told it to him.

He said, "My name is Rodgers."

"Yes. It was on the ticket, remember?"

He nodded. "So it was. Do you mind if I call you Madelyn?"

"As you wish."

"Will you have dinner with me tonight, Madelyn?"

Her eyes widened as though with surprise.

"Sorry to be so blunt, but I don't want to lose track of you."

She lifted her brows. "Why not?"

106

"That should be obvious. Would I have asked you out unless I wanted to become better acquainted?"

"I suppose not. Very well, you may pick me up at seven, Mr. Madden."

"Won't you call me Rodgers?"

She gave a small assenting nod. "Rodgers."

"Where do you live?"

Again, she seemed surprised. She gave him an address in the Pontalba buildings.

He arrived at her apartment promptly at seven o'clock. She was ready, but she invited him in. She had rented the apartment furnished, but had added some personal touches of her own. He glanced about with interest; she had done well on what he knew to be a very limited income. He walked to the window and looked out over Jackson Square.

"Good view from up here," he commented.

"I like it. I love the French Quarter."

"Yes, it's picturesque."

She came over to stand beside him. "You feel you are back in history up here. You can almost pretend it's a hundred years ago."

He turned to look down at her. "I shouldn't think a modern young woman would see much appeal in that."

She bestowed on him the dazzling smile that wrought havoc with his emotions. "I suppose I'm old-fashioned. Perhaps I was born a century too late."

Rodgers shook his head. "No, you were born just about right, I'd say."

Their eyes met and held. She glanced away finally. "Maybe we should be going, if you're ready."

He took her to Antoine's. From her pleasure, he guessed she had not been there before. He'd noticed a kitchen in her apartment and suspected she took most of her meals in to save money.

Leaving the restaurant, Rodgers suggested a stroll to settle their dinner, and Madelyn started off toward the right.

"Not that way," Rodgers said. "You don't want to walk down Bourbon Street, do you?"

She lifted teasing eyes to his. "Don't you? Most tourists do—male, at least."

"I've seen it," he confessed. "I don't want to take you there."

Her hand tightened in the crook of his arm. "Thank you, Rodgers. You couldn't pay me a greater compliment."

They walked slowly to Royal and up to St. Peters Street where they cut over to Chartres and Jackson Square.

"When do you have some time off?" Rodgers asked. "I'd like for you to show me the museums."

"We could go tomorrow afternoon. If that's all right."

"That's fine. I've seen a few myself, but it's more fun to go exploring with someone."

They entered the park. There was a chill in the air and Madelyn drew her coat closer around her. "It will soon be Christmas," she commented.

"Yes. One week from today."

"Will you be going home, then?" she asked.

They were walking slowly. He gazed down at her and made his decision. "No, I'll be here for Christmas. My business in New Orleans won't be finished that soon."

She glanced up into his eyes and said nothing.

Rodgers called for Madelyn at her apartment on Tuesday afternoon. The day was cloudy; earlier it had rained.

"Wrap up," Rodgers advised. "It's turning cooler out."

She put on an all-weather coat over her suit. "This will be warm enough. It's cool for New Orleans, but that's still not cold."

"Well, where shall we go first?"

"There's a museum across the square, in the Pontalba building, one in the Cabildo, and another in the Presbytere."

"All right, let's take them in order. We'll start across the square. I haven't seen that one at all."

It took them an hour and a half to complete the tour of these three. They saw furniture of another century, heavy and carved of dark wood, well polished. Plainer, lighter woods had been used for bedsteads and chests to furnish the quarters of slaves. They studied the clothing of the past and the oil portraits. Doll houses were exquisitely made, the tiny furnishings exact replicas of the period.

"Nothing turned out by machine today compares with this," said Madelyn, enchanted by a doll house fashioned to represent the real home of its young mistress.

"No," Rodgers agreed. "This was an age when men took pride in work. Life wasn't easy but toil was rewarding to the soul."

"What a lot we've lost with our modern conveniences!"

Rodgers nodded. "More than we realize, I'm afraid."

"But can we go back to that era?"

He sighed. "I don't see how. And some things we wouldn't want to go back to—disease, hardship. We must try to recover the values of the past, though."

They saw the death mask of Napoleon and stared at it for some time, trying in imagination to reclothe the features with the flesh and blood of the real man. They saw prison cells where pirates had been bound in chains. Going on from the museums to Royal Street, they toured a house with slave quarters preserved as they had been in the late 1700's.

Their tours took the entire afternoon. When they had completed the last one, Rodgers said, "I'm afraid I've worn you out. And you must be starved. Let's have something to eat."

"I have a casserole at home. Come and share it with me," Madelyn suggested.

"Wouldn't you rather I took you out?"

She smiled up at him. "No. Really, I'd like to fix it for you."

Rodgers grinned. "Okay. I won't quarrel with home cooking."

The apartment after dusk was cozy and homey. Madelyn tied an apron around her dress, completing for Rodgers the picture of domesticity. She brought out antique candlesticks she had found in a shop in the Vieux Carré and inserted handmade candles. The meal was delicious, and afterward Madelyn brewed coffee and brought it in to where Rodgers sat, thoroughly relaxed.

"I can use this," he said. "I'm about to fall asleep right here."

She gave him a faintly teasing smile. "Dull company?"

"You know better than that. You're looking at a deeply contented man."

"That's flattering."

"It wasn't meant to be flattery. You know, I never believed that old saying—the way to a man's heart——"

She laughed nervously. "You hardly know me, Rodgers."

"Oh, I wouldn't say that. We've had several dates and we've talked a lot. I think I know you pretty well."

"I don't know you very well," she said, avoiding his eyes. "I don't know, for instance, why you are in New Orleans."

"I've told you. I'm here on business."

"But what sort of business?"

"I'm a lawyer. I'm here in connection with a case our firm is handling."

Their glances met. Her face was still. "What sort of case?"

"I'm afraid I'm not at liberty to go into that with you, Madelyn. Why does it matter?"

"It doesn't," she said quickly. "I was curious, that's all."

He smiled. "Very feminine. I do have a legitimate reason for being in town. I'm not a crook, nor am I some sort of shady character."

"I didn't think you were. I didn't have to ask you here."

"No, but I'm glad you did."

She smiled. "More coffee?"

He shook his head. "I've had enough. I'd better be leaving, it's getting late." He got up and touched her face in a gentle caress. "Thanks for the tour and for dinner."

"You're welcome."

Rodgers picked up his jacket and because he was a bit too relaxed, he was careless with it. The coat slipped from his hand. He caught it with a reflexive grab that knocked his papers loose from the inside pocket and scattered them onto the rug. Madelyn's picture fell face up between them. For a moment they both stared down at it, then Rodgers bent to retrieve his scattered possessions. He put everything, including her picture, back into his pocket and put the coat on.

Madelyn looked at him. "So, what are you going to do?"

When he didn't answer, she said, "I knew who you were as soon as I knew your name, of course. Your father has represented Mr. Brewster for years. I thought you had come for me, that you'd tracked me down, but then when you didn't say any-thing about it, when you simply dated me—well, I didn't know what to think. I still don't. What's your game, anyway?"

"I have no game," Rodgers said.

She looked at him hard. "Are you going to try to say you met me by accident?"

He shook his head. "No, I was looking for you."

"Well, then?" Her mouth curled sardonically. He didn't like it, or the hard defiance in her eyes. "How did you find me?" she asked.

"I went to Chicago, talked to your aunt."

"She doesn't know I'm here."

"She thought you might be."

Madelyn shrugged. "So, you tracked me down. I don't sup-pose it was too difficult, I'm not used to running. What are you going to do now? I won't change my mind, you know."

"Change your mind about what?" Rodgers' eyes narrowed thoughtfully.

"That lousy plan your father dreamed up."

Rodgers frowned in surprise. "What plan?"

She turned away from him. "Still playing games? I imagine you are quite adept at fooling a girl when you want to, aren't you? You certainly fooled me."

"What plan?" Rodgers repeated.

She turned back. "If you don't know, then why were you looking for me?"

"You're a material witness. Brewster claims you took care of his books, and that if money is gone that should have been paid to the government, you are the one who's stolen it."

She nodded. "Yes. That's the plan."

"What *plan?* I don't see any *plan* there. Except on your part, if you did steal the money."

"I didn't. Brewster knows that. And so does your father."

"My father doesn't know either way for sure. That's why he wants to talk to you."

"Who told you that?"

"He did."

"Then he's lied to you." She considered him a moment. "Maybe you really *don't* know what's going on."

"I'm afraid I don't. Suppose you explain it to me."

"Mr. Brewster cheated on his income tax returns. I'm the one who didn't know the score. Do you think he wouldn't check the figures of a mere secretary before signing his name to the return? He must have changed them later. He always put the forms in the mail himself."

"There was a time, then, when you didn't see the returns? Before they were mailed in?"

"Yes."

"All right, go on. What was this plan?"

Madelyn sat down and looked up at him, the hostility gone. "You really don't know, do you?"

"No, I don't."

"Sit down, Rodgers. Please."

He did so. Madelyn said, "It was your father's idea. At least I understood it to be."

Rodgers nodded. "And what was the idea?"

"That I would say I'd made a mistake on the returns. The books were all right."

"They aren't now."

"I know. Brewster falsified them, but they were all right as I'd kept them. That will probably be impossible to prove though."

He agreed.

"I was to admit to making a mistake. For that I would be paid five hundred dollars. Brewster would pay what was owed to the government and that would be the end of it. Apparently, though, your father decided it could not be made to appear a mistake. He decided I should admit to—well, embezzling would be the word for it, I guess. I would pretend to give the money back; of course I would not actually pay anything to Mr. Brewster. He would reimburse the government with appropriate apology, fire me but refuse to press charges, and secretly pay me three thousand dollars for my trouble."

"Hm. I see. So why did you run away?"

"Because I didn't want to go along with their scheme! Does that really surprise you? I might escape jail, but what of my

112

reputation? How would I ever get another job? How could I face anyone?"

"All right. You didn't go along with the idea, you ran. That wasn't very smart. They're pinning the blame on you anyway. Your running away looks like a confession."

"I can see that now. I don't know how I can persuade you to believe me. I have only my word to offer you as proof."

"You have a bit more than that to offer."

"How do you mean?"

"There's my father. I know him, you see. This all sounds very like him. I've been a first-class fool. But just now we don't need to be concerned with that. And then there's you. I had trouble all along seeing you as an embezzler."

"Did you?" She smiled.

"I don't think I could feel the way I do—well, we needn't go into that either, just now."

"What can we do? How do I get out of this mess?"

"You'll have to go back and tell the truth, Madelyn. You'll have to appear as a witness against Brewster."

"Oh."

"Don't worry, it'll be all right. We won't go until after Christmas. We are going to enjoy the holiday right here in New Orleans."

"What about your father? What does he think you're doing here all this time?"

"He thinks I'm looking for you." Rodgers grinned. "It's going to take me another week to find you."

Madelyn laughed. "Then I invite you to have Christmas dinner with me. How's that?"

"Fine. And let's go to church somewhere together Christmas Eve."

He got up for the second time. "I really must go. You're not to worry. I'll see you tomorrow."

"Thank you, Rodgers, for believing me."

He looked down into the candid eyes. "I couldn't have done otherwise, Madelyn."

"Nevertheless, I'm very grateful."

"I don't want gratitude. When I get you out of this mess, I'll tell you what I do want." He took hold of her shoulders and kissed her lightly on the forehead. "Good night. Get some sleep. I'll call you."

13

Rodgers was filled with intense anger as he left the girl's apartment. His father had played him for a fool. He'd had no idea of changing the way he practiced law. He had never intended to reform. It was all a trick to entice Rodgers into joining the firm. He had employed the only method that would have worked—an irresistible appeal for help. Rodgers realized now that he had turned his back on the Hollis Creek Church for nothing. He had broken his commitment to God and to Wilbur Wickham for nothing at all.

He was angry at his father, but more than that he was disgusted with himself. There was no excuse, he felt, for his stupidity. Especially after Wickham had tried so hard to warn him.

He covered the distance to the hotel quickly with his long-legged stride. The walk was too short, however, to dissipate his anger. He passed by the entrance, continuing on to Canal Street, then turned right there. He kept moving, losing track of time and distance, driven by a restlessness that made inactivity impossible.

Fatigue slowed his pace at last and he halted to look around him. The surroundings were unfamiliar. He had no idea how far he'd come or in which direction. He shook his head slowly like a man waking from deep sleep. His anger was gone; he was only tired now. Well, that was good; he'd be able to sleep. Tomorrow he would have to decide what to do to help Madelyn. He passed a street sign—he was on Canal Boulevard. He turned about and walked slowly in the direction of the hotel. When a cab cruised up alongside him, he hailed it.

The hotel operator gave him the message that his father had telephoned. Rodgers decided that he could use the late hour as an excuse to delay returning the call until morning. He needed some time to sort out his thoughts and decide just what he would say to his father.

But he had no chance to return the call in the morning. He overslept and was awakened by his father calling him.

"Where have you been?" the elder Madden asked abruptly. "Did you stay out all night?"

Rodgers propped himself up in bed and switched on the lamp. The draperies were closed and the room was dark. He glanced at his watch—eight-thirty.

"No, I got in, but it was too late to call you."

"What were you doing? Oh, never mind. You seem to be living it up down there at my expense. I don't begrudge you your pleasures so long as I get what I want. Where's the girl?"

"I've got a good lead," Rodgers said. "Give me one more week, I'll have it wrapped up."

"Next week's Christmas."

"I know. I'll be home right after. I expect to have her by then."

"You'll spend Christmas in New Orleans? Your mother won't like that."

"I'm sure you can explain it to her," Rodgers replied. "Why waste the fare home when I'm this close?"

Madden sighed. "Okay, Rod, but you'd better not be stalling. I'd better get something out of all this. You've been in that hotel a month already, you know."

"You'll get as much from me as I've gotten from you."

"What kind of crack is that?"

"I mean if we're partners, we trust each other. I level with you as you level with me."

"Are you saying you think I haven't leveled with you?"

"Now what gave you an idea like that?" Rodgers queried. "Do you want to forget about the girl?"

"No! I don't know what your smart remarks mean, but get this straight—you try to cross me and it'll be the worst mistake of your life. You understand that?"

"Couldn't be clearer," Rodgers said amiably.

"All right. Don't forget it. I'll expect you back here on the twenty-sixth. With the girl."

"Yes. You have my word on that," Rodgers said.

"All right. Just so we understand each other. Good-by."

"Oh, Dad!" Rodgers said.

"Yeah, what d'you want?"

"Merry Christmas."

"Oh. Yeah, sure. Same to you."

On Christmas Eve Rodgers and Madelyn found a Protestant church and attended services together. It was midnight when the service was over. They came out into the clear night and began to walk slowly in the direction of Madelyn's apartment.

"I'll try to find a cab," Rodgers said.

"No, don't." She tucked her arm in his with a smile. "Let's walk. It's not too far."

"It's a little cool."

"I want to. Please."

He grinned down at her. "I can't refuse you anything."

Presently, she said, "Rod, were you always a lawyer?"

"No, not always. Once I was a little boy."

"I'm serious. I have the feeling that you are something else."

"Why?"

"You don't seem to belong to the profession of law."

"Well, you're right. I'm a minister."

"Then why——?"

"Let's just say I had planned to be a minister, but I was side-tracked for awhile."

"And you are a lawyer, too?"

"Yes. I took law first. I passed my bar exams and then I studied for the ministry."

"It's fortunate for me that you went back to law."

"Oh, you'd have gotten out of this anyway."

"I'm not so sure. And if it had been any other lawyer besides one with your moral principles, it might have turned out as it did with your father."

"There are other good lawyers. Many of them." He glanced down at her as they walked. "I'm fond of you. That can't have escaped your notice entirely."

"No, it hasn't—entirely."

"In fact, fondness is a pretty weak word for the way I feel. I'm in love with you, Madelyn."

"Are—are you sure, Rod? Maybe you only feel sorry for me."

"No, I don't feel sorry for you. Why should I?"

"The trouble I'm in——"

He smiled. "I've met women in trouble before, believe it or not." He said slowly, "Actually, I think I must have fallen in love with you before we met."

She stared at him. "What?"

"I had that picture of you. I took it out to look at often. Finally I realized it was not altogether because I was tracking you down."

She laughed. "That doesn't sound like you. You aren't the type to fall in love with a picture."

"I know. Sometimes I surprise myself."

At her door, he bent to kiss her. "I won't come in, it's too late. Merry Christmas, my darling."

"Merry Christmas. Rod, I love you, too."

"Do you?"

"Very, very much."

He kissed her again. "We'll get married just as soon as this mess is over and I can reorient my life. I don't have much to offer—I'll have to find a church to serve. And there won't be much money for a while. Not too much—ever. Ministers aren't rich, you know."

"I know. We'll have God and each other. We'll make it all right."

"Yes, we'll make it. Oh, my darling, I love you so!" He held her and said, "Madelyn, I have an old and dear friend who's a minister. Would you mind very much if I asked him to marry us?"

"Of course not."

"He'll be glad I've found you and that I've gotten my feet on the ground at last."

"I can't believe your feet were ever really off the ground."

"I've been badly mixed up. But it'll be all right now. I can see a purpose in it all, and I know where I'm going at last."

Rodgers had a traditional Christmas dinner with Madelyn. It was cold out and raining, but in her apartment they were comfortable and happy.

"Everything would be perfect," Madelyn said, "if only we didn't have to go back tomorrow."

"Don't worry about that. I'll take care of everything."

"What will your father say?"

"I'm not worried about that. He should worry about what I'll say. You've done nothing wrong, and you have nothing to be afraid of."

Harvey Madden was at the airport to meet them. His eyes searched Rodgers' briefly before passing on to the girl. Rodgers ignored the inquisitive glance.

"Dad, this is Miss Wythe."

"How do you do," Madden replied politely. "You've caused us quite a hunt, young lady."

"We'll talk tomorrow," Rodgers said, "Miss Wythe is tired. Where is your car? I want to drive her straight home."

"Home?" Madden queried.

"Yes. Where she lived before. The girl she was staying with will put her up."

"But I want to talk to her. We can go to my office."

"Tomorrow," repeated Rodgers firmly. "We'll let her rest tonight."

His father accepted that, finally. They drove to the girl's apartment in silence. Rodgers left his father in the car while he carried Madelyn's bags in for her. She fished a key out of her purse.

"Whew! Thanks, Rod, for sparing me tonight."

"I'll call you in the morning," Rodgers said.

"What time do you want me to see your father?"

"You may not have to see him at all. I'll talk to him to-night. I think he will be content to drop the whole matter."

"I don't like to put it all off on you."

"It's better that way. Don't worry. I've told you I'll handle everything."

In the car his father asked, "What did you get out of her?"

Rodgers stared straight ahead through the windshield. Snow was starting to fall. So far the streets were only wet, not icy.

"The truth."

His father glanced at him. "She admitted taking the money?"

"No." Rodgers switched on the wipers. "She admitted you and Brewster tried to bribe her. When that failed, you framed her."

"That's a lie! Don't tell me you *believe* that?"

"Yes, I do. It's just the sort of rotten scheme you would come up with."

"You've fallen for that girl, that's your trouble!"

"Shall we call in the police and let them make a thorough investigation of Brewster's financial affairs? I think the missing money will turn up someplace, probably in stocks and bonds. And his handwriting on the books where he had to change her entries can probably be detected, too."

"I'm sure Brewster won't want to carry it that far, going to the expense of proving the girl a thief. He had hoped to settle this quietly. He has no wish to be vindictive."

"I was sure that would be the way you'd see it," Rodgers said drily. "You and Brewster have hearts of gold. Incidentally, I'm tendering my resignation. I'll clear my things out of your office in the morning."

Madden sighed. "All right. I won't try any longer to interest you in law."

"I'm amazed that I was such a fool!"

"Look, Rod, let's just drop it, huh? No recriminations—from either of us."

"All right. I guess that's best."

"It's the only way."

They drove home in silence.

Rodgers had dinner with his mother and Alicia. His father didn't come down from his room.

Alicia smiled with a twinkle of fun in her eyes and asked, "Did you find that girl?"

"Madelyn Wythe? Yes, I did."

"She's not in any trouble, is she?".

"Depends upon your point of view," Rodgers replied.

"How do you mean?"

He smiled. "She's going to be your sister-in-law."

"Oh, Rod! You're getting married?"

"You've found the girl you want to marry?" Mrs. Madden asked.

"Yes. To both your questions."

"Show her the picture, Rod," Alicia coaxed.

He took it out of his wallet and handed it to his mother. She studied it closely for a long moment. "She is very pretty, Rod. When do we get to meet her?"

"Soon."

"And when are you going to marry her?" Alicia inquired.

"Soon, too."

Rodgers pled fatigue to parry further questions and went to bed early. Tomorrow he would talk to Madelyn and to Wilbur Wickham. Tomorrow his life would swing back on course as he re-oriented himself to the work he loved. Tomorrow he could plan a future with the woman he had chosen.

The following morning he had the office to himself while he cleared out his things. Miss Hamilton was reticent; perhaps she had been instructed to give him a wide berth. It didn't matter, for soon he would be gone. He had a few books of his own to collect, files to turn back in to Miss Hamilton, and notes to destroy. He was through in an hour. He called Madelyn to tell her that she was in the clear.

She sighed with relief. "Oh, Rodgers, I'm so glad. You're marvelous."

"Sure I am," he said with a chuckle. "Don't you forget it."

She laughed. "No. I won't."

He rang off after arranging to see her for dinner. Next he called Wilbur Wickham. A strange voice answered the telephone at the manse.

"May I speak to Mr. Wickham, please," Rodgers requested.

There was a hesitant pause. Then the other man inquired, "Could—may I ask who's callin' him, please?"

"This is Rodgers Madden."

"Oh—oh, Mr. Madden. I'm Joe Daniels. We've met, if you remember?"

"Of course, Mr. Daniels."

"Well, I—I don't know how to tell you this—Wilbur Wickham is dead, you see. He died December twenty-third. We buried him on Christmas Day. I tried to get in touch with you. Your father said he would be sure you got the message."

Rodgers felt numb.

"No. No, I didn't get your message, Mr. Daniels."

"Well, I'm sorry. I didn't know where to reach you——"

"How did he die?" Rodgers asked flatly.

"It was pneumonia. He had a bad cold at Thanksgiving and it just never got better."

The *cold!* Rodgers remembered, of course. He had told Wickham to take care of it, and then engrossed in his own affairs, he had not even checked again with the old man.

"He was in a coma toward the last," Daniels continued. "I have a letter he wanted you to have. He wrote it when he was taken to the hospital on December eighteenth. Could you come by the manse to pick it up?"

"Of course. I'll come in a few minutes."

"I'll be here. Good-by, Mr. Madden."

"Good-by."

Wilbur *dead*. Rodgers put his head in his hands in an agony of shock and regret. His father purposely had not told him. For a moment anger burned with the quick, bright flare of a match, then as suddenly went out. What good would it do to reproach his father now? Wilbur was gone. Nothing could change that. He realized painfully how much he had looked forward to telling Wilbur of his decision to return to the ministry. He had anticipated the older minister's encouragement and guidance, his forgiveness. Too late now for that.

A quiet knock came at the door. Rodgers lifted his head. "Yes? What is it?"

"May I come in, Rod?"

"Yes. Come in."

Madden entered and for a moment father and son surveyed each other with gravely questioning eyes.

Rodgers said, "Sit down. I'm just finishing up here."

"There's no hurry—but I guess you are in a hurry. I don't blame you for that. I don't blame you for anything, Rod. That's what I've come to say. I'm sorry."

"Yes. So am I."

"Rod, I'd like for you to forgive me, if you can."

"I just tried to call Wickham," Rodgers said.

Madden's lips tightened. His face became a shade paler. "I see."

"Do you? Have you any idea how you've hurt me by this? You knew how much I loved him. Can you conceive of what learning of his death now—too late even to attend the funeral—has done to me?"

His father looked at him, a measure of pain coming at last into his eyes. "Yes, son, I think I can. What can I say to you? I'm sorry. But how futile it is to say so now."

"But you do mean it?"

"Yes. I mean it. I won't expect you to forgive me, Rod. I won't ask again."

Rodgers rose. "I can't say it's easy for me to forgive you. I think it'll be even harder to forget. But I'd like to try, Dad." He extended his hand.

His father took it slowly, almost in disbelief. "I don't know what to say, Rod."

Rodgers smiled. He felt as though a weight had lifted inside him. "I don't think we need to say anything just yet. Later, we can talk. Perhaps in time we will have the relationship we should as father and son."

Madden gripped his hand with a wordless nod. At the door he turned back. "Thanks, Rod."

"Good-by, Dad. I'll see you at home in a little while."

The roads were clear driving to Hollis Creek. The snow that had fallen the day before covered the ground and cast an aura of magic over the otherwise bleak countryside. The sky was overcast, waiting. Rodgers felt simultaneously an uneasy tension and an inward peace.

He drove into the churchyard and walked from there over to the manse. Daniels opened the door for him before he knocked.

"Come in, Mr. Madden."

"Thanks." Rodgers stepped into the quiet house. It was clean and neat. Fresh flowers had been arranged in the parlor. Already though there was an air of emptiness, of vacancy to the place. And yet it would not remain empty. It was a manse. There would be another minister. Rodgers sighed, feeling the weight of his grief for Wickham.

"I'm sorry," Daniels said. "I could have found an easier way to tell you, perhaps. I'm afraid I wasn't very gentle."

Rodgers shook his head in denial. "You were gentle enough. There is no gentle way to break the news you had."

The men sat down. Daniels took the letter from his pocket and handed it across to Rodgers.

"He left a will," Daniels said. "You're to have everything he owned. Which isn't much. Mainly it's his books."

"That's a great deal. He has a good library."

Rodgers opened the letter. It began:

My Dear Son in the Faith,

I shall not be able to wait for you to get here, I fear. That doesn't really matter, though of course I do wish that I could see you once more. The things I have to say to you matter greatly to me, however.

First, do not grieve for me, Rod. I am not grieving. To this end has my life been directed — that I might see my Lord. I can say with the Apostle Paul, "My desire is to depart and be with Christ." One thing only concerns me, my son, and that is your future. I am sorry that I must leave

124

you unsettled in it. I have prayed for you constantly that you may, like the Apostle Peter, turn again.

Tears started in Rodgers' eyes. He read on.

> I feel assured that you will. When that happens, do not waste time in futile regrets. Repent, accept forgiveness, and get on with the work to which you were called. Know that I myself have long ago forgiven you — indeed if there was really anything to forgive. We are all human and being human, we make mistakes, Rod. You were honest in your mistake.
>
> I have made a will. Regardless of what you do with your life concerning the ministry, I want you to have my few earthly possessions. My books will prove valuable to you, I believe, whatever your vocation.
>
> Farewell, my beloved son. We shall meet again, as you know. Until that time I remain your sincere friend,
>
> Wilbur Wickham

Rodgers folded the letter carefully and put it into his own pocket.

"Would you like to see the grave?" Daniels asked gently.

"Yes. I would."

They walked through the snow to the cemetery. Wickham's grave was as yet unmarked. Snow covered the fresh mound. Rodgers stood beside it, dry-eyed and silent.

"We're gettin' a marker," Daniels explained. "It will be engraved with his name, the dates, and the first stanza of that hymn you love. He sang it almost every Sunday after you left."

Rodgers repeated it softly.

> O Love that wilt not let me go,
>   I rest my weary soul in Thee,
> I give Thee back the life I owe,
> That in Thine ocean depths its flow
>   May richer, fuller be.

Daniels said, "That's a beautiful hymn, but for me it doesn't have the meaning it did for the two of you."

"That's understandable," Rodgers said. "For each of us there's a particular hymn or verse that strikes a responsive chord in the soul."

Daniels gave the younger man a warm smile. "I think Wilbur liked it because of you. He was very fond of you."

"Yes, I know. And I of him. I'm sorry I wasn't here."

"He talked about his church before he died. It was his hope to the end that you would return here to serve."

Rodgers looked down on the fresh grave. "And is that the wish of the congregation, too?"

"Yes. They want you. Do you mean you'd consider it?"

"The people of this church are very dear to me. If they'll have me, I certainly shall accept."

"Thank you. They'll be pleased. The Martins particularly have been praying for this."

"How are the Martins?"

"Tom's a changed man with his son home. The farm's prospering."

"And Mary Jane?"

"She's taking a business course. Doing real well, I hear. Should make somebody a good secretary in a few more months."

"I'm glad."

Daniels grinned. "I hear she's right popular with the fellows, too. Might be she'll make a wife before she ever does a secretary. But I reckon that's a risk you take, educating girls."

Rodgers smiled. "Still, she won't regret the education, I'm sure." He turned toward the church. "Is the door unlocked?"

"Yes. We never lock it. That was a strong point with Wilbur. The church must always be open. 'Who knows,' he said, 'when a lost soul might want to enter?' "

"Yes. Yes, indeed. If you don't mind, Mr. Daniels, I'd like to be alone for awhile."

"Of course. I'll be at the manse if you want to stop in before you leave."

"Yes, I will."

Rodgers entered the church. The heavy sky outside made the sanctuary dim. He walked forward to touch the keys of the organ, remembering the first day he had stopped by the church, when Wilbur Wickham had played their hymn. He turned and his eyes came to rest on the pulpit from which he had delivered his sermon. Tears started in his eyes. Wilbur had requested that he not mourn. He would honor that request; only now, briefly, he gave in to his grief and wept.

The worst of his anguish spent, Rodgers knelt beside the pulpit and lifted his face toward the window where he could see the heavens.

"Father, I'm home," he cried. "O God, I've come home!"